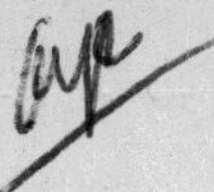

From: Delphi@oracle.org
To: C_Evans@athena.edu
Re: forensic psychologist, Francesca Thorne

Christine,

As I told you last week, I've put Francesca Thorne on our case. If anyone can confirm the links between Arachne, the Queen of Hearts and Marion's mystery prisoner, it's Chesca.

The last few Oracle agents I've put on Arachne's trail have encountered dangerous situations. Francesca's an Athena grad, and I know she can hold her own, but I would feel more at peace with her involvement if she had backup on this investigation. You mentioned your great-nephew during our last call. Is he still between positions after recovering from that bullet he took in the line of duty? He's just the man Chesca needs.

Would you contact him about going to Boston?

D.

Dear Reader,

It was an honor when Natashya Wilson asked me if I would be interested in contributing to the Athena Force series. As an avid fan of all things Bombshell, I loved the idea behind the characters, conspiracy and cover-ups at the Athena Academy, and I knew I would have a blast getting to know Francesca Thorne up close and personally.

I loved Francesca's commitment to digging deep into her prey's psyche and unraveling clues to piece together a profile of motive and opportunity. I've always been a fan of forensic psychology, and watching Francesca maneuver her way around obstacles was a thrilling ride for me, one which I hope you will enjoy, as well.

Please stop by www.loriamay.com to say hello and share your thoughts on Francesca and Will's Athena adventure!

Lori A. May

Lori A. May

MOVING TARGET

ISBN-13: 978-0-373-38977-3
ISBN-10: 0-373-38977-9

MOVING TARGET

This edition published by arrangement with Harlequin Books S.A.

Visit Athena Force at www.eHarlequin.com

Printed in U.S.A.

LORI A. MAY

has never confronted a serial killer, chased a suspect down an alley or broken into an encrypted government computer. Yet she still considers herself a go-getter, thriving on the less dangerous excitement in her own life, created by making things up and putting pen to paper. Her real-life adventures are more likely to include exploring an unfamiliar city, trying new restaurants and experimenting with photography and visual arts. For the latest news and events, plus reviews, contests and more, visit www.loriamay.com.

To my personal support team and cheerleading squad:
Mom, Dad, Zaida and Chris.

ACKNOWLEDGMENTS

Special thanks to Jay Poynor and Erica Orloff
for their enthusiasm, support and friendship—
and middle-of-the-night e-mails!

To Natashya Wilson
for asking me to join the Athena Force series
and to Stacy Boyd for her editorial eye.

Chapter 1

He pulled tight around her throat, choking her.

He didn't say anything. He didn't have to.

Francesca Thorne was accustomed to gathering information from criminals in what wasn't said, whether it was through a look, a nervous tic despite attempts to mask such a giveaway, or simply a change in vocal pitch.

It was what an opponent did not say that aided in the patchwork of piecing together a personality. Her role was simply to watch. Observe. Filter the subtleties of the subconscious into her puzzle-solving mind.

Whereas she would normally calculate facial expressions and measure the pupil dilation of her suspect, waiting for a flinch to reveal so much more than well-selected words, the opportunity had not been given with this particular hunt.

Instead, she had to count on the sound of his breath, the weight of his grasp as he held one arm tightly around her neck, choke-holding her into submission with her back facing him, unable to meet his eyes.

He had snuck up on her.

Though she had returned to the scene to analyze its meaning, determine why the killer had chosen this location for his latest victim, Francesca had not been counting on his presence. Not yet.

His attack had caught her by surprise.

The killer had demonstrated an odd pattern of returning to the scene of his crimes only to enact another, but in between he always committed a murder at a different location. That was his MO. Or at least the first five murders had suggested as much with his leapfrog style.

One location, then another, then back again.

By their calculations, he should have been somewhere else preparing to commit the sixth. She had chosen to come here with the hopes she could piece something together about his selection process, quickly enough to determine where the next crime would take place.

But his MO had changed.

It was inevitable he would switch it up.

Knowing his back-and-forth actions as she now did, he would have been caught sooner or later, with the FBI knowing to stake out his previous playground. And, really, it was just child's play for him.

"You like taking risks," she said, holding her voice steady, not allowing even a shred of fear to show as the pressure of his grip grooved over her esophagus. "Yet you refuse to show your face. Slightly passive-aggressive, don't you think?"

When in close contact with a serial killer, Francesca Thorne—lauded forensic psychologist for the FBI—pulled no punches in calling it as she saw it. That included tempting fate by asking somewhat dangerous questions, or igniting a suspect's volatile nature. It was a trait for which she was known.

Setting herself up for increased risk was part of the job. The very act of trying to diagnose the criminal mentality meant opening up a whole world of unknown psyche. But it was within that very process that she was able to collect the critical data needed to prove or disprove a profiling theory, much like a forensic scientist would test the boundaries of physical evidence.

In this case, mocking her captor only made sense. Her action would cause a telling reaction on his part.

His breath, moist as he exhaled along her ear where his lips barely slid over the curve of her skin, was calm, masking any trace of anger or excitement.

With his body held snug against hers, she could begin to create an image of his physical presence in her mind. Not the specifics such as eye or hair color, but from his stance she could estimate his height.

From his breadth against her, she could make calculations of his weight.

It was the nonvisual clues he gave, such as his scent, his body temperature, and his reaction to her teasing that would matter most. And with what little headway they had made with this case, these variables would not only help her plan a maneuver away from his grasp, they would also lend a hand in solving the identity of their prey.

She closed her eyes, banning their sense from interrupting her analytical intake. She filtered in a deep breath, letting the combination of scents register within.

Ignoring the aroma of a nearby Laundromat, bypassing the scent of rain in the air, she centered on the slight trace of chicory and breathed it in from the cuff of his sleeve.

The sleeve itself belonged to a blue-collar worker. She could tell by its wear and tear, the threads of cheaply made industrial fabric worn with sweat stains and something dark—oil, perhaps?

She inhaled deeply, pinpointing the smell.

It was oil. Like that used on machinery, perhaps in a factory or even an auto mechanic shop.

Knowing what trace evidence could do for fine-tuning such variables, Francesca made a minuscule movement within her captor's grasp, aiming to transfer even a hint of the physical evidence to her body. If she made it out of there—when she made it out—the lab would be able to study every fiber of her clothing, each thread where this man had left evidence of his identity.

"It won't be that easy," he said, no doubt presuming

her maneuvers were an attempt to flee his grasp. "You and I are friends now."

That was it. The first time his voice made contact with her sense of hearing. She listened to each syllable he projected, to what was being said and how, not once overlooking the quiet beat of a pause between each word he selected.

"Is that what you wanted from them? Friendship?" she asked, opening up dialogue with the man her team had been tracking for several weeks.

It started with one body, as it usually does, but it quickly became obvious someone was on the hunt for more action with the discovery of the second victim.

The most disturbing element to the case was that he was a smart criminal, relatively speaking. He knew how to disguise himself, how to leave little trace of evidence, and thereby bring the forensics team to a standstill, waiting…for him to mess up.

"I am not who you think I am," he said, his one arm holding tight against her neck. The other arm reached around, wrapping against Francesca's midsection as though this were a perfectly natural position for him. There was no trembling, no jittery movement. He felt completely at ease clenching his ownership around her body.

"Then tell me," she said aloud while inside her mind a thousand thoughts scrambled for a plan on how to make her move.

An agent from the Baton Rouge resident office had accompanied her to the crime scene, though he remained at the car guarding the scene from the outset. His presence would do her no good at such a distance. "Tell me who you are. How you see yourself."

He scoffed at her. "What—you some kind of shrink?"

Francesca registered the curve in vocal pitch, his agitation showing fluctuation in the short response. She had hit a nerve, without trying much at all. His own suggestion was fueling his irritation, based on one simple request for him to explain his assumed persona. And now she would use it against him.

"I like to help people, with their thoughts," she began, noticing the heat rise from his body.

The dewy evening air, signaling an early April rain shower was on its way, carried his scent swiftly to her senses, and she was able to detect a rising pulse. "I could be your confidante. Listen to what you have to say. I bet you feel as though no one understands you, but perhaps I could. If you let me."

It didn't mean she would like him or appreciate his actions, but Francesca could use her skills in understanding human behavior to at least empathize with him, see what it was that motivated him to strike out against humanity. It was something for which she strived every day, with every criminal she came across.

Her pursuit had begun as a young child, during events she rarely cared to recall. It was those events, however, that prompted her pursuit of understanding why people do the things they do, and led her to study behavioral science.

At first it was simply a curiosity, one she explored

through watching others, even as a child. Then she became enthralled by the lessons learned in psychology classes at the Athena Academy for the Advancement of Women, a prep school that encouraged the study of such scientific interests.

By the time Francesca earned her graduate degree in forensic psychology, profiling personalities had become an obsession. One for which she was quickly recognized within the field, handling seemingly impossible cases for the FBI, even those reaching far beyond her home base in Richmond, Virginia.

"I don't need a shrink." His voice, increasingly harsh, told her she needed to make a move. Fast. His agitation would only escalate and there was only so much fire she wanted to tempt within him. He was, after all, a serial killer.

One who baited young women, dragged them out to isolated buildings, beat them, assaulted them and finally killed them.

Above all else, Francesca needed to remember that one obvious trait within a killer's personality—they liked to kill.

Although her own preference was for capturing her suspects and wielding information about their psyche, to analyze and put them through a tougher sentence than death, she had to admit to having a simpler fantasy as his tongue traced the outer edge of her earlobe.

Though she wanted to put an end to his existence when he said, "Maybe you have something else I want."

There had to be a better way for her to flee his entrapment and bring him down.

Killing was what she studied, not what she did. There had to be something she could do to not only escape his captivity, but also ensure he was stopped from ever committing another crime again.

And then she spoke.

"Maybe you have something I need," she said, playing on the notion he was a sexual predator and using that to her advantage as she slowly, carefully reached her hand around to settle into the small groove of space between her behind and his crotch.

Earlier, as he attacked her in surprise, the man had quickly removed her handgun from her person and tossed it far from her reach.

But what he didn't know was about to hurt him.

Under the guise of giving him what he wanted, Francesca began to move her hand over the small bulge in his pants, twisting her gesture until her palm faced the small of her back, and while she listened to his breathing accelerate under her touch, she slowly moved one finger, then the next, into the gap between her flesh and her jeans until she felt it.

"I do, don't I?" he asked of her.

"You most certainly do," she cooed to egg him on, as she cautiously slid out the small knife from the sheath buried in the back of her pants. Within a heartbeat, she twisted its edge into him, stabbing the blade into his left hip as she said, "Your DNA."

Caught off guard by her attack, the suspect stumbled back to let the moment register, but he quickly set off on foot.

As she began the chase after him, slowing only to pick up her discarded handgun, she let out a contained breath, one she didn't realize she had been holding.

Not familiar with this abandoned dumping ground of rotten buildings and wasteland, Francesca called for help by shooting one bullet into the ground, knowing this would alert the watchdog FBI agent that something had gone terribly wrong.

They had not expected to encounter their suspect today. This was simply an outing to gather mental evidence, its sole purpose to comb the area and turn thoughts inside out, hoping to accumulate enough information to pinpoint where the next victim might be saved.

Then it occurred to her.

Why would the killer come here, switching up his MO if he knew the feds were on the scene? And if he didn't know he'd be in mixed company, why did he return to this place?

To kill his sixth victim, she thought to herself.

Francesca stopped in her tracks at the realization.

Changing her direction, she ran back to where the criminal had discarded her personal belongings, and combed through the weeds to find her cell phone. As she did, Agent Martin caught up with her location, slightly winded.

"That way," she cried as she frantically dialed the

number for the field office. "He's run off through there, but I think we may have a body on site."

Her words filtered through the air as Agent Martin ran off to chase down the unknown suspect. Until now, without a name, a list of potentials or DNA findings, this case had proven frustrating.

Which was exactly why the Baton Rouge team had called in the expertise of Francesca Thorne.

They needed a profile, and that's what she aimed to provide, but now she also had a knife with his blood on it. A personal identification he had failed to ever leave at the scene of a crime, but which could be added to the file in the hopes of matching it with other physical evidence compiled from the series of events and seal the deal of his conviction.

She quickly informed the field office of their estimated whereabouts, and added, "I'm heading into the vacant building on the south-east side of the lot," to ensure they would know where to find her.

It was from this very direction the man had come, stepping up behind her as she walked through the gravel along the outside of the building. He must have heard her from inside.

Had she even remotely suspected his presence, she would have taken every precaution to avoid the rumbling sound of loose gravel, but hindsight was a waste of time right now. There could be a sixth victim within the vicinity, and if so Francesca swore to find her.

As she stepped lightly through discarded broken

glass, rusted hardware, and rodent feces, Francesca's attention was momentarily diverted by an incoming call from her cell phone.

She recognized the distinctive ring assigned to the caller and her breath caught, knowing Delphi was attempting to contact her. The mysterious communication leader from Oracle, a secret intel operation for which some Athena Academy grads had been recruited for their unique skills, would not expect Francesca to answer.

Instead, the simple act of hearing Delphi's call would instruct Francesca to either check her secured e-mail account, or to return the call from a landline. Only in a pinch would the two ever communicate over the cell. Francesca simply wouldn't trust its promise of privacy.

Though she was curious about the purpose of the call, Francesca maintained her focus on the case at hand. She would contact Delphi after this scene was declared clear, but for now her main purpose was to locate a possible victim—one she hoped was still breathing.

"Thorne?"

Francesca followed the direction of the voice. It was one belonging to Agent Sharland of the Baton Rouge team, which meant her call had been answered swiftly.

"In here. Watch your—" She grinned as Sharland nearly stepped a foot flat into something nasty as he rounded the corner, meeting her inside the decrepit building. "Step."

His grimace replaced the opportunity to say thanks, as Francesca continued her search for a body.

Within the abandoned building, one formerly used for a textile business if she recalled correctly, there were a number of floors to clear, but within each only a select number of hallways to snake through.

"We got him. Martin's fine, too," Sharland said, settling Francesca's unanswered question. "How about you? You okay?"

"Shhhh. Listen," she said in a careful whisper. As they stepped along through the concrete landscape, there was something that caught her attention.

It could be the slight chatter of a sewer rat, the nesting of a bird, or it could be something else altogether and Francesca wanted complete silence from her fellow Fed in identifying its whereabouts.

Sharland nodded in acknowledgment of her request as they followed the sound, faintly coming from a shadowed room down the hall.

Through the doorway a small stream of natural evening light shone down against the damp concrete underfoot, and as she cautiously stepped into its illumination, Francesca noticed the small barred window facing the direction of where she had been attacked.

From inside this room, their suspect would have been able to watch her movements, gaining the upper hand in sneaking up on her as she collected intellectual data.

A muted shuffle to the left caused her attention to narrow in on a darkened corner, and as she moved closer to the sound, Francesca breathed a sigh of pained relief.

Agent Sharland expressed what she was thinking

that very second. "He must have been distracted by you out there, before he took the time to—"

She cut him off by shaking her head. She knew it was likely true, but there was no need to fill in the details with the young woman lying before them, curled and hunched in a darkened corner, clinging to her beaten life.

Had Francesca Thorne not insisted on visiting the site to analyze the killer's selection process, victim number six would have been dead.

At the Baton Rouge field office, Martin, Sharland, and several of the other FBI agents were combing through the newfound information, gathering a case against the man they hoped would be prosecuted for a series of murders, and one failed attempt.

The evidence always had the final say in making a charge stick, but with what they'd encountered and the crime that had been stopped in its progress, the killer hadn't had time to cover his intentions. His DNA would certainly help, as well as the additional trace being collected off Francesca.

She stood still, careful not to disturb the process of collection, while a local team member combed through her hair, and removed all trace of the man's presence on her body.

"My things?" she asked when the protocol was complete, determined to sign on to her laptop and check her awaiting e-mail.

Delphi had signaled for her attention and though the criminal case against this serial killer was far from over, Francesca's role in it had come to an end. She could now offer full attention to the call from Oracle.

After her personal belongings were returned to her, Francesca took a moment to shake hands with the various agents she had come to know in this recent, but brief assignment.

"We asked for the best," Sharland said, offering a firm shake and a rare smile. "I'm glad they went one step further."

"I'm sure your work is just about to begin," she said, signaling her departure with a casual salute to the brow. Never one for goodbyes, Francesca preferred to keep it simple.

Outside, she crossed the street to a cozy café that advertised a wireless high-speed Internet zone. While waiting for a taxi to take her to the airport where she would catch the earliest flight back to the familiar territory of Richmond, Virginia, Francesca settled into a booth, nursing a cup of black coffee, and then typed in the password to access her e-mail account, ready to view Delphi's message.

It was a short one, at that. Knowing more information would be awaiting her arrival back home she couldn't help the curiosity about what activity was calling her into action.

The message simply read *assignment for you,* which was enough to pique her interest.

To anyone else this would likely seem vague and cryptic.

But Francesca knew all too well what was being asked of her. An assignment from Oracle implied she would be working with highly sensitive information.

More important, Francesca knew, the request was one she would promise to execute and make top priority.

Chapter 2

Within the comfort of her own apartment, surrounded by the familiar, Francesca settled into the window seat with her laptop, taking a moment to peer down at the busy street below her. In the heart of the downtown core, the view afforded her the greatest science experiment of all—watching people in their natural habitat.

After graduate school, and her training with the FBI in Quantico, Francesca was stationed within the Richmond field office to handle some of the toughest profiling cases ever to cross an agent's desk.

While that usually led her to work with murderers, and she had a knack within the specialty of fingerprinting serial and spree killers, her profiling skills extended to hunting down a variety of cases handed to her. Serial offenders, no matter what the charge, were some of the trickiest individuals out there when it came to the professional world of crime. But it was always the tough ones Francesca thrived on solving, loving that sense of accomplishment that would arrive when a case closed. Even though the success of one case was short-lived with the assignment of another case to crack, those minuscule moments were worth it all, reminders that her work was valued not only within the FBI, but as a productive role in society.

No matter where an assignment took her or how difficult a case she was dealt, it was her modest home retreat where she worked best, enjoying the calm it could bring in between cases, and the quiet it could shed on an overactive mind.

It was something coworkers had commented on far too many times. Francesca's inability to leave work at work, and save the moments at home as some sort of spa-like sanctuary. Sure, it all sounded great in theory. Turning off the working mind entirely, however, was easier said than done.

This, though, was nothing to complain about, as far as she was concerned. Her mind had a way of mysteriously working, even in her sleep, and putting together the puzzle pieces of profiling cases was something she lived for. It was her passion. Her obsession. Her purpose.

And really, Chesca had so little of a social life outside of her colleagues and keeping in touch with connections made through Athena Academy, that her downtime away from work was…well, mostly focused on work. It was a stark contrast to the socialite home life she was reared in as a child, that's for sure. But working the big cases had become her life's carrot. It's what made her feel whole.

Smart enough to realize life couldn't be all work and no play, Francesca did her best to make her home environment as comfortable as possible, so that she had the best of both worlds.

It may have been considered a working playground by some, but to her it was a haven away from the office chaos. A place to concentrate. Formulate ideas. Connect the dots. And it was comfy as hell.

Though the domestic environment of her childhood home was of museum quality—harsh lines, stuffy upholsteries, over-the-top everything—Chesca preferred comfort over style when it came to home fashions. Usually this applied to her personal wardrobe as well. What was the point in having a pricy settee that no one would dare touch? Not that she entertained guests often. Which further emphasized the point of making sure her abode was the most comfortable and casual it could be.

The ultrasuede couch was her most beloved furnishing in the small but ample apartment, nearly seeming overstuffed and oversized for the one-bedroom, second-floor unit. But the collection of throws, mixed-and-matched textures of pillows, and a well-placed shag carpet all catered to the sense of feeling swept off her feet.

Perhaps it was the deliberate contrast of her upbringing that led her to prefer comfort, practicality and function. Whether she was working on an all-night caseload, or drifting off to late-night infomercials, it didn't matter so long as she could put her feet up, let her back slide into cushiony softness, and feel…at home.

Despite her reputation for being career-focused, Francesca was often regarded as a "what you see is what you get" kind of person, her simple lifestyle contrasting with the often-complex cases she'd encounter in her work world.

Alex Forsythe, fellow Athena grad and FBI forensics colleague to Francesca, had often said she admired this trait in her friend, knowing no matter how complicated the world around them could get sometimes, there was nothing better than counting on a good, solid friendship that was as clear as day, and hassle-free.

Which is exactly how Chesca preferred to keep her living situation. Hassle-free. While a substantial section of her urban apartment was dedicated as a workstation, stacked with files, case histories, and tools of the trade, this never cluttered her comfortable environment, or took over the meaning of her home.

Bringing work home, and letting it clutter her life were two very different things, and Chesca always made sure that no matter how tough a case she was working on, she knew when to file something away for the night, and how to file something as "out of sight, out of mind."

That's why it was so important to her to feel completely at ease in her no-nonsense style, and let the warm earthy tones of her chosen décor act as a backdrop for her office away from work. Plush decorative pillows, simple but soft fabrics, and a carpet that hugged her bare toes as she paced back and forth mentally dissecting criminal evidence allowed her to relax, focus, and get the job done while casually clad in cotton boxers or her favorite jeans.

The bare bones but earthy warmth of home was often all she needed to zone into whatever her mind needed to tackle.

But there was little peace within her mind as she sat in the window seat today, watching people below, their faces just a glazed blur as her mind reeled around something much more pressing.

The assignment from Oracle.

Since returning from the case in Baton Rouge, Chesca had managed to have a full day to unpack, unwind and await further information from her extracurricular employment.

Delphi had sent a message informing Chesca a courier would soon be delivering further information pertaining to the assignment, and the only additional hint of what was to come was the mention of something very important to Francesca. Something that would hit close to home with the many women associated with Athena Academy and all those who fought to see it succeed.

She would be profiling the notorious blackmailer Arachne, determining whether she was one and the same as the Queen of Hearts assassin.

The name Arachne was enough to raise the blood pressure of just about any of Francesca's social circle. With her cover blown, it was now understood Arachne was behind the recent student kidnappings in an attempt to bring down the Academy.

Putting a face to the name would be Francesca's goal, not only as part of her assignment from Oracle, but to finalize the fight her fellow Athenians had been trying to win for far too long.

Quite honestly, it was an honor to have been assigned this case by Oracle. The intel organization could have called on any of its recruits for such an assignment, but for some reason Delphi had made her selection, and Francesca was not only flattered, but personally determined to do whatever it would take to be of assistance.

Francesca wasn't the only Athena grad to be recruited by the network, though she had little indication of who the others were, what their roles were, or why they were selected. It was rare to hear of a fellow agent's work, though it wasn't entirely unheard of.

For everyone's safety, she presumed the details of the operation had to be kept secret. The one thing all participants knew, though, was the extreme importance of the intelligence gathering it conducted, as it did its part in fighting for justice even when standard institutions such as the FBI, NSA or CIA backed away.

No one really understood how the information was distributed within Oracle. Only that when an agent had carried through with an assignment, a full report was to be given to Delphi, the enigmatic handler of the operation.

Though Francesca had her suspicions from time to time, she didn't admit to having a clue of who Delphi might be in reality. Of course it was a code name. But if she was meant to know, she would in time.

For the most part, Francesca had let her analytical mind piece together what she imagined the inner workings of the organization to be, but there was little she knew as honest-to-goodness fact, since she rarely had any contact with Delphi, and never personally came into contact with other agents from the organization.

The few times Delphi had requested Chesca check into something, it was taken care of within hours. She knew from the intake process the types of information she would potentially be handling, but until now she had never been assigned a full case. No matter how long it took, or what the case required of her, Francesca swore this assignment deserved her full and immediate attention.

Before agreeing to send the initial case file, Delphi confirmed with Chesca that she would be able to step away from her regular duties at the FBI for a few days, if not more.

There was no question.

Even if Chesca didn't have a lengthy stockpile of comp days to her credit, there was no way she'd turn down a full assignment from Oracle. Especially one pertaining to the ongoing battle between Arachne and the Athena Academy. Between her curiosity and her thirst to handle something unique and pressing to the intel organization, this elite opportunity was what she craved. What she had trained for. And despite not knowing the full details of where it would take her yet, for now, Francesca knew her help was needed.

Oracle needed her. The Athena Academy needed her.

She was proud of her experience at the Academy. Grateful for the opportunity afforded her, providing for her the chance to truly work to be the best she could be, both as a young, eager student in her younger days and all the way into her blossoming career.

Thinking back on what an incredible gift the education at Athena Academy was to her, and countless other talented and uniquely gifted young women, Francesca couldn't help but smile over the memories. They also gave her opportunity to think fondly of her time spent long ago, growing up in the company of others who had as much drive, as much conviction, as she herself possessed. Others she considered dear friends.

Despite having years of positive memories to reflect on, Francesca knew all too well the serious and unfortunate occurrences Athena and her graduates had been subjected to recently, not the least of them happening during the past year or so.

Athena Academy may have been regarded as home to many, but to some…it was something to fight against. Maybe there was something to that old cliché, about people fearing the unknown or the simple things that just weren't understood by the masses.

The Athena Academy for the Advancement of Women had been born to create opportunities, and contribute something positive to society, and yet there were those who couldn't help but try to destroy what others helped build.

It saddened Chesca. How a handful of unscrupulous individuals had worked to tarnish the very place she called home, the respectable names she considered family.

Thinking of that home, the place where she'd felt most at ease in her childhood, and in becoming the woman she was today, Francesca had the urge to touch base with the one Athena sister for whom this assignment held the most urgency.

"Allison. It's been a long time," she said, grateful to hear the familiar voice over the phone.

Though she wouldn't confess to the Oracle assignment, and knew very little of what it entailed as of yet, Francesca wanted to speak to the daughter of Marion Gracelyn, founder of Athena Academy.

More than a decade had passed since Marion's death, but it was only last year that her daughter Allison, along with forensic scientist Alex Forsythe, had discovered Marion was being blackmailed at the time of her murder. Allison had already been through so much with the murder of her best friend Rainy, that Francesca felt the need to reach out to her fellow Athenian.

"Chesca? Don't tell me you're actually at home for once."

She smiled at Allison's friendly tone and good spirits. With what she'd gone through, well…some wouldn't be able to handle such tragedies with Allison's grace and courage. She was truly someone to admire.

"Not home for long, I'm afraid. But I had to hear your voice. See how you are."

"I know with you it won't be what I say, but how I say it, so let me make sure I get my intonation correct when I tell you it's nice to hear your voice, too," Allison said. "Do I pass?"

"Flying colors," she said, though already fast-forwarding her thoughts to less amusing concerns.

Not knowing completely what Allison knew about the full assignment given to Chesca, she had to tread lightly on the subject. Thus, she approached her question at an angle. "I understand you've been in contact with Beth. Any chance you reclaimed my books for me?"

Allison laughed. The more recent reputation of Bethany James might have been one of professional gambler, but even back in the days at Athena Academy, young Beth knew how to run a poker table. A natural loner, likely due to her upbringing on the streets by a hustling—but loving—father whose lifespan was cut short by an enraged murderer, poker was one of the few social activities Beth would participate in at the Academy.

While Francesca, too, was one who preferred to keep to herself most of the time, the opportunity to play alongside Beth offered up a glimpse into her character, where her true personality was most revealed, and for this Francesca took every chance to get to know her elusive classmate. Even if it meant losing several coveted books to the power player, such as one of Chesca's favorites on quantum physics.

They were the same age, challenged by the same rigorous program at Athena, but Francesca Thorne and Bethany James were very different, at least to outside eyes.

Beth came from the high-risk life of street gambling, and Francesca emerged from a blue-blood battlefield where money was the root of anything worth caring about. Well, at least in the eyes of her parents. Francesca never fit the mold when it came to that, and she still felt the ramifications to this day from her disappointed mother and father.

Yet on some level, there was a common denominator between those two teenage girls. Both highly intelligent, both focused on striving for their personal best, there was something more that bonded the two of them. They had lost someone dear to them at an early age. And now, they had experienced the same feeling of loss again with the continued revelations surrounding the murder of Senator Marion Gracelyn, a mentor with a passion for the empowerment of women who was sadly removed from this earth, all too soon. And for all the wrong reasons.

"That Beth. She nailed you a few times, didn't she? Good thing we put an end to that," Allison said, reminding Chesca of the many times Beth had been busted for her poker nights.

"You think you put an end to it," Chesca clarified, "but you know she's an unstoppable force."

"Aren't we all?" Allison asked, her tone letting Chesca know she spoke through a smile.

It was true. *A force to be reckoned with.* That was how graduates were now proudly referring to themselves amongst one another, pleased with the many varied accomplishments each individual class had to offer the world.

Of course, not all Athena grads turned to a profession of law enforcement or politics, as evident with the gambler Bethany James and reporter Tory Patton, to name a few.

One thing all graduates had in common, though, was their intent to fight for justice in one way or another, and when it came to vindicating one of their own, there was no force like that of the Athena Force.

"Then let me ask you," Francesca said, refocused on the original intent of the phone call. "Do you think the person blackmailing Giambi is the same person who was blackmailing your mother?"

Through her quick glance at the files Delphi had sent over for Francesca's return to Richmond, she'd already pinpointed a few flags to follow up on.

Salvatore Giambi, owner of the Sapphire Star Casino in Monaco, had recently come forward to the FBI citing his involvement with the Queen of Hearts. While she had plenty of information from Delphi, and could obviously follow up on this incident through files at the Richmond office, she needed to hear the opinion of Marion's daughter.

"It seems worth pursuing. Beth did some snooping while at one of Giambi's gambling parties. You may want to check in with her for more details. Anyway, he had been making regular payments into a Puerto Isla bank account, but no one has made a withdrawal in three years." As Allison paused, Chesca listened to the quiet air over the telephone wires.

"Allison? How are you holding up?" While the assignment would become the number one priority for Francesca, she didn't want to overlook the sensitivity required when discussing Marion's death with Allison.

Though rarely emotional, and definitely hard to peg most times, Allison had to be facing unimaginable demons. A person cannot rise above such trauma without feeling conflicted along the way.

"You know me," Allison said, and though Chesca wanted to laugh, feeling like she didn't know Allison half as well as some of her other Athenian sisters, she knew this was not the time to be argumentative. This was Allison's way of letting her know she'd rather not get into a deep discussion about it. "You know where to find me, if you need help in an official capacity—or otherwise for that matter."

A skilled NSA programmer and mathematician, Allison Gracelyn would no doubt come in handy at some point down the road, and despite her mysterious personality she was always upfront about her support for her fellow Athenians.

"I do, and I'm sure I will," Chesca said, accepting the conversation as over.

After their pleasant, but brief, goodbyes Chesca continued to study the files revealing Salvatore Giambi's activities and began to prepare her mind for taking on the assignment. The request from Delphi was to assemble a profile on the blackmailer Arachne, and to determine whether she was one and the same as the Queen of Hearts assassin.

Having kept up with the inside investigation of Marion's death through the Athena Academy Web site, as well as through occasional conversations with former classmates, Chesca had already heard a bit about each of these personas.

Though she hadn't personally dived into the investigation until now, she had given a good deal of thought as to why anyone would want to put a stop to the existence of the Athena Academy for the Advancement of Women, and ultimately Marion Gracelyn.

At the time of the academy's creation, there was a tremendous outcry from politicians, government forces and pretty much any outlet for power, as there was concern such an institution would cause havoc to so-called traditions and standards of training. Though anyone who knew Marion would have known her intentions were simply to offer keen young women the same advantages, and the same opportunities, as men in what was at the time a male-dominated world.

Even now, despite every "equal opportunity employer" claiming to level the playing field, Chesca knew all too well the reality that women had to work that much harder to gain the same respect, the same foot in the door, when it came to so-called equality.

That's why she'd focused so hard on her academics, fought off youthful urges to socialize when every one of her college classmates were headed out for a night of fun. To get anywhere in this world, Francesca Thorne knew she had to channel her drive, passion and motivation into one focused fusion of settling for nothing less than excellence.

It was that internal focus which elicited her recruitment by Oracle. It was that passion which would propel her to uncover the truth about Arachne and compile a profile that would lead to solving this bit of tragic Athenian history.

There was nothing about this profiling assignment that caused worry or concern for Francesca. She knew her skills, recognized her strengths and knew when to let others assist her, and with the personal nature of this case, she knew she'd do whatever it took to get the information Delphi requested of her.

That included doing something she did not particularly look forward to. Making a trip to Boston.

Though a beautiful and historic city, and no doubt the best place to start off her investigation, seeing that both

Giambi and this Queen of Hearts character hailed from there, the city was also home to a few other unscrupulous individuals.

The Thorne family.

Though it made her stomach cry out in knots when thinking of going back to her own hometown—something she hadn't done in some time, thankfully—Chesca knew she had to do whatever she was called to do. That included accepting that uncomfortable feeling of treading on home turf.

With her simple style and no-nonsense knack for packing, Chesca did a once-over to make sure she had everything she would need for the next few days. A basic wardrobe, the Oracle case files, and the reservation number for the car rental she had arranged just hours ago.

Looking at the concise travel ensemble, it all seemed straightforward enough. But Chesca knew there was nothing simple about returning to the blueblood neighborhoods in which she'd been raised prior to Athena Academy. Not when it was that very hometown she was so pleased to outrun in her youth. Thankfully, since this was an investigation into the criminal underbelly, Chesca would likely be trekking around a few locales less than familiar to her family's grassy estate.

Not that the Thorne family was innocent when it came to committing social crimes of their own. Infidelities, stock-trading tricks and business activities that sometimes seemed less than level in the eyes of their daughter, Chesca knew her father Dorian and mother Abigail were less than perfect.

Yet despite their various affairs, sexual and otherwise, the Thorne family had a stellar reputation amongst the silver-platter crowd, one that irked the very soul of Francesca. How is it, she often wondered, that people with such power choose to abuse it and use it for their own personal gain?

That was often the case, though, she knew. For blueblood parents or high-stakes criminals, the game was always the same. Those who sought out personal power and couldn't care less about who got in their way. This was the world she was going back to, the one she'd so gratefully left years ago.

The only thing that triumphed over the sick feeling in her gut was knowing that when it came to solving cases, sometimes the best place to start was the beginning. And, as far as she could tell, for Giambi and the Queen of Hearts, their history began in Boston.

As she locked her apartment door behind her, Chesca breathed a sigh of anxiety and trepidation. "Then Boston, here I come. Oh, there's no place like home."

Chapter 3

Despite the ease of travel an air ticket would afford her, Francesca had elected to rent a car for the nine- or ten-hour drive to Boston from Richmond.

She wanted the maximum freedom and convenience of swift maneuverability, knowing wherever the case led her, she would be able to get moving from one destination to the next in no time, without the hassle created by waiting to board planes.

She loved driving. The open road, complemented by the ability to process thoughts along the way, offered an opportunity to digest some of the case file information Delphi had sent over, and provided Chesca the chance to think through some of the history of this situation.

Sitting between strangers on an overly crowded

popular flight was no place for her to analyze sensitive information. But the opportunity to travel through a few landmark destinations like Washington, Jersey, and Connecticut in the sporty, bright-red Ford Edge she'd rented, was perfect for letting her mind wrap around the beginnings of this puzzle.

Or at least of this particular piece of the puzzle.

Sadly, the Athena Academy and those who supported its existence and purpose were the target of many unfortunate events. For decades, attempts had been made to bring down the Academy, and some of those activities had left bitter results, such as the murder of founder Marion Gracelyn, and that of Rainy Miller Carrington.

But little could be done to dent the conviction of the Athena Force. Nearly two years ago, three graduates had successfully foiled a plot to assassinate Gabriel Monihan, the current president and also, Chesca mused, the significant other of Athenian Diana Lockworth. Though they kept their relationship out of the limelight, they were an incredible match for one another. Chesca and her fellow Athena sisters were truly pleased for Diana and Gabe.

Love like that was hard to find, Chesca knew, never having quite found that perfect someone for herself, but still believing it was possible. Against her parents' wishes, though, she knew whoever sparked her inner romantic would definitely not be someone whose sole purpose was carrying on socialite affairs and uniting for the basic premise of carrying forward historic family names.

Chesca wanted a relationship like Gabe and Diana's.

She was envious of what they had, but that didn't equate with jealousy. She was happy for them, and the genuine item they had become. Their relationship was real, something they could count on.

Thankfully the assassination plot on Gabe was shut down so his political career was secured, and his romantic affair with Diana was able to blossom.

It was those moments of happiness for her fellow graduates that Chesca loved to hear about. Between cherished memories of her youthful days at the Academy, and the inspiring careers and personal successes of her friends, there were some truly great moments to celebrate.

The darker moments, like this ongoing struggle with Arachne, were the moments that fueled the drive and passion of Athena's graduates, the moments where their skills and expertise were best put to use.

As was the case last year, with Alex and Allison solving Marion Gracelyn's murder and discovering that she had been blackmailed. The truth about Arachne would be found out, with both the Oracle network and Athena women not willing to let anything further happen to bring down what they all held so dear to their hearts.

Throughout the drive, Francesca was able to piece together some of the basic background information on the affairs conducted between Arachne and Giambi.

Between the case file she received from Oracle and the conversation she'd had with Allison, Chesca knew they were each much bigger players in this game than any of them would have originally anticipated.

The ongoing hunt for justice regarding this matter was fortunately being handled by those Chesca could trust. Beth James, gambler extraordinaire, had recently uncovered the connection between Arachne and Giambi, and as Chesca reached her halfway point, she decided to take Allison's suggestion and dialed a distant friend to exchange information.

"Going back to your roots, are you?" Beth joked after the initial pleasantries of connecting with her former classmate.

"I wouldn't exactly say that. But, Boston seems to be where the action is, and thus that's where I'm headed."

Beth laughed with a familiar chuckle. "So no family dinners, I take it?"

"You know who I consider my real family," Chesca said.

"Hear, hear. So, what do you want to run by me?"

Chesca was pleased to be able to connect with Bethany. Though she was a skilled blackjack player and a high-stakes poker natural, she donned a disguise each time she played, and kept her identity safe from casino bigwigs. Those who were aware of how well she made her living, however, kept a keen eye out and rooted for whatever persona Beth presented in any televised games.

It was a rush, imagining the sort of life Beth must lead, though Chesca knew all too well there was a good deal of personal vendetta involved. With Beth's father dying the way he did, at the hands of someone who had been dealt a bad hand, it had become Beth's personal crusade to bring down known cheaters, but she'd never herself succumbed to the dangerous lifestyle that no doubt tempted far too many a player in Vegas.

"Giambi and Arachne," Chesca said, getting to the point. "Who's blackmailing who?" It was half asked in earnest and half as a mockery of what these foolish criminals imagined they could get away with.

"You know the meat," Beth said. "Giambi's been making some hefty deposits to a bank account in Puerto Isla on a monthly basis for years. Quite the coincidence he's also been spared by the IRS, don't you think?"

Opening the driver's side window just enough to let in some air on the damp spring afternoon, Chesca turned the volume up a notch on her earpiece. She didn't want to miss anything Beth had to offer.

"And, I have it on good authority," Chesca said with a smile, "Giambi came forward to the FBI to cover his assets."

"You got it. But, Chesca, listen up." And she did. As her friend took on a more solemn tone, she wanted to pay extra attention to any helpful bits of information. "He needed to do so for serious protection. Whoever was sent to attack him was doing a pretty good job. His car was blown up, for one thing, and that wasn't the only attempt made on his life. So," Beth warned, "whatever you're up to, make sure you watch your back."

"Will do. And Beth, am I right in this? Giambi referred to his blackmailer as the Queen of Hearts?"

"You're right," Beth offered, letting Chesca in on a bit more of Giambi's background. "He was suspected of trying to firebomb an Arizona prisoner back in 1968, but walked away from the charges. It's not impossible that prisoner was the Queen of Hearts *and* Arachne."

To take down some notes and give Beth her undivided attention, Chesca took an off ramp to stop for a moment in a safe location. "But Giambi had bigger problems."

"Right. According to him, in his confession of sorts, he admitted the prisoner was his blackmailer and he tried to kill her, but that's not all."

"Go on."

Chesca's pen was writing as fast as her friend could speak. Amongst the details Beth shared with Chesca, one thing stood out amongst the rest. "Giambi suspects his blackmailer may have been a CIA agent."

Making a mental note to run this information by Delphi, Chesca was reeling.

If what Giambi confessed was true—though Chesca had known more than one criminal to say anything to get a safe haven—this mercenary, this Queen of Hearts, could have been intrinsic to the many attempts against Athena Academy.

Was it really possible one individual could have so much power, so many connections, as to be involved in such a conspiracy?

Chesca let the thoughts formulate in her head as steady traffic flowed by her on the expressway. She was parked securely off to the side, tucked into a carpool parking lot away from the chaos of the road, but the rumble of the cars couldn't compete with the traffic in her mind.

What a history of corruption, Chesca thought.

For Giambi to try and kill his rival way back in 1968 meant their relationship went back even further. And he was still running from his blackmailer. Chesca had that gut feeling deep within her that whoever was capable of taunting someone for so many years would be capable of so much more.

She was beginning to get a sense of what she was up against.

But she was never one to tremble in the face of evil. Chesca had seen evil minds at work before, and this wouldn't be the last she would encounter in her career.

"Thanks for the info, Beth. You've been a great help."

As Bethany James wished her success in her investigation, Chesca returned to the road, eager to get her game on in uncovering the truth about Arachne and the Queen of Hearts. She'd put an end to the question: Are they one and the same?

It would only be a matter of hours until she arrived in Boston. There was so much to do, so many things to sort out. She took a moment to just breathe the air filtering through her window, letting the damp cool spring air refresh her senses.

It seemed any road trips Chesca embarked on were work-related, and for a moment she wondered what it would be like to just take off from work, abandon all sense of responsibility, and travel the countryside with her hair in the wind, music blaring, and nowhere in particular to go.

She laughed, thinking it was impossible for her hair to blow in the wind, with the very short, and very—thankfully—low-muss, no-fuss closely cropped style she preferred. Not one to primp and spend hours of time in front of the mirror in the morning, she had long ago let go of the notion that there was a style to her dark brown hair. The look had grown on her to the point that she became annoyed when even an inch grew in before she had time to make a stop at the barber down the street from her apartment. A barber, for sure, when she discovered she could get the same cut there for a third of the price at one of the fancier salons in the downtown core.

And that whole notion of shooing off responsibility? A road trip might be something she would enjoy, but Chesca was never one to leave work that far behind her.

Perhaps it was the hard-core academic training she'd received prior to joining the Athena Academy. Or perhaps it was the discipline she'd honed while studying amongst the nation's best. But Chesca prided herself on her ability to focus, set her goals, and go after them with the voraciousness on which her reputation had been built.

Really, she had only ever had one slight pitfall in her academic career, and that had nothing to do with learning or taking on a scholarly challenge. But it had everything to do with why the Academy had recruited her at that time.

That memory had already crossed her mind more than once since receiving this assignment from Oracle.

Returning to her hometown of Boston caused her stomach to turn with mild anxiety, and it wasn't only her scandalous family that caused her to react as such.

There were other memories there that Chesca preferred to keep in the past. But the past had a funny way of catching up with the present, Chesca knew all too well.

Despite making every attempt to have a normal childhood amongst a family focused on greed, popularity and materialistic gain, Chesca didn't have it quite so easy as her schoolmates might have thought.

Never would she deny that she'd had every opportunity afforded to her that money could buy, and for most of what her parents could provide for her, she was extremely grateful. She knew well enough not to look a gift horse in the mouth, and she was fully aware she had it pretty darn good compared to some of her schoolmates.

Between being raised by emotionally vacant parents and not having any siblings to count on around home, Chesca had been unprepared for some of the social life she experienced outside of the formal dinners and fancy parties of the Thorne residence. It was difficult for her to connect with "normal" kids, whose families led happy lives and weren't the subject of gossip for every other parent in the school district.

But that was nothing compared to what she'd endured in fifth grade. Nothing could have prepared her for that.

One of the few friends Chesca had made on the playground was kidnapped, raped and killed.

It stung the core of Francesca, not understanding how something like that could happen with school officials, guardians, and passersby being unaware.

Not only was it a blow to lose a friend to such a tragedy, there was no explaining how the criminal had hidden his identity so well from others.

The murderer was a schoolteacher.

One who had previously had respect and been highly regarded amongst the community. He let them down. He let Chesca down. She had enjoyed his manner of teaching, felt he had a great sense of humor and camaraderie with the students, and worst of all—she'd felt safe with him.

In fifth grade, to be such an age, and lose so much faith and trust in adults, in teachers… Chesca was traumatized.

How could someone like that be revealed as a pedophile who had killed more than once?

The counseling sessions began, then multiplied. No matter how many times a shrink tried to help Chesca heal those wounds, however, there was nothing anyone could do to take away the hate and disappointment she felt toward society.

Even now, so many years after the fact, Francesca Thorne could not make sense of what it was that drove some people to do such horrific things. As a child, it wounded her. But it also propelled her. To survive. To never let anyone get so close to her under such false pretenses.

To pay attention.

To observe and notice hints of personality traits that may subtly indicate something was at work other than what was at face value.

Though she hated admitting it, that unfortunate incident might well have been the foundation of how and why she grew a passion for digging deep into profiling people. It was part of her nature, perhaps, because she felt it had to be, from a very young age.

The old adage that from tragedy rises good, may have had some merit. Perhaps, had it not been for her personal experiences as a child, Chesca might not have taken such a keen interest in human behavior, psychology and social sciences.

Perhaps, had it not been for her own personal experience, she would not have taken her work to heart and excelled to the point that the teachers at Athena Academy noticed her gift almost immediately.

No matter what it was that had led her to the Academy, Chesca was grateful. And being reminded of her roots, the vast differences between her upbringing in a socially corrupt environment and in the nurturing environment of the Academy, was enough to fuel her senses and give her the push to settle the score made against that in which she believed.

She would find out the truth behind Arachne.

She would uncover the mystery of whether Giambi's

CIA blackmailer was the same woman who was doing everything in her power to destroy the Athena Academy for the Advancement of Women.

She would ignore, as much as possible, the reminders of her home life while here in this city, and focus on her task at hand.

Was Arachne also known to some as the Queen of Hearts?

Chesca vowed to find out the truth.

For Oracle. For her fellow Athenians.

For herself.

This was not a social visit. This was about work.

And though her upbringing would argue otherwise, her stay in Boston was going to be anything but a tea party.

Chapter 4

After checking into the hotel, Francesca had quickly set up an appointment at Boston University before calling it a night. The drive had worn her out physically, but her mind was circling through the wee hours of the darkness as she contemplated the magnitude of this assignment. Then again, some of her best work was accomplished when in sleeping mode, letting her mind relax into a state of purity, where facts filtered and formed patterns, leaving her with a refreshed feeling of alertness upon waking.

During that next morning, Chesca made a list of things she wanted to accomplish, and she got right on the phone to start the wheels turning.

In a modest briefing with Delphi, they caught one another up on where Chesca was and what her initial plan of attack would be. Delphi agreed to dig up information on the possible connection between their blackmailer and the CIA.

Though she didn't know exactly how Delphi found access to such highly sensitive government information, Chesca was assured she would have CIA files couriered to her when it was safe to do so. In the meantime, Chesca had an appointment set up to get the case rolling and she felt confident in her to-do list.

Once she had the hotel room feeling as close to home as possible for the next day or so, sorting out her work items from her wardrobe, Chesca set out again in the sporty Ford Edge to make the first stop in her investigation.

Despite being on familiar ground, Chesca couldn't help but notice how much the city had evolved since she'd lived here as a child. She rarely found the time or made the effort to come back for a visit, except for the odd "required" social gathering she made appearances at as the sole offspring of the Thorne family.

Now, seeing the city as though she were a stranger visiting from a far-off land, Chesca felt bittersweet about her return. Focusing on the details of this assignment would be her saving grace and keep her from dwelling too much on the past.

Her first stop was the Computer Science Department of the Charles River Campus, where she would see if she could evoke some fond memories of someone who may have had the goods to be recruited by the CIA.

Allison had mentioned the apparent computer skills their suspect possessed, and thus Chesca had set up an appointment with the current department head.

While it was unlikely she would find anyone on campus that actually knew their suspect personally, given the time frame they were dealing with, it was worth a shot. And, wasn't that what student records were for? If the computer science nerds couldn't dig up history, no one else would have a clue.

Driving along Storrow Drive, Chesca took a moment to glance at the familiar territory and fight off her recurring historical demons.

This was not her personal alma mater but she'd always had a fondness for the institution. It was, in America, the first university to open all its curricula to women, and in some ways that reminded her of the mission of Athena Academy.

Though the views along the banks of the Charles River reminded her more of her playful youth.

In the summer after graduating from Athena Academy, Chesca had a few weeks to spend at home in Boston prior to attending an internship program in Quantico.

It was before she had actually set foot on her own college campus, and rather than witness the social niceties around the Thorne residence, Chesca found solace on a patio of one of the many coffeehouses on Commonwealth Avenue, and watched students go about their fevered summertime activities.

It was the perfect opportunity to spy on people her

age, watch them flirt in hot-weather flings, shop for seasonal trends, and just be in the moment. It was also the closest Chesca got to living that life.

Though vicariously so, it was her way of participating in the excitement. In reality the patio table she sat at was often covered in texts and notebooks, even in the heat of summer. Of course it was her choice to bury her nose in books, but there was the odd time, like driving into the campus on this beautiful spring day, that occasionally made her nostalgic for a youth she hadn't entertained.

While her youngest years were of the quieter, more studious sort, Chesca made some quality friends to share her teen years while attending Athena Academy. And despite what most of them would like others to believe, it wasn't all academics and exams.

Those girls, though dignified in their behavior, knew how to have a good time amongst themselves. They enjoyed their wonderful and massive backyard, and when all else failed, they easily made up a myth or two about mysterious men shadowing the landscapes of the academic grounds.

Chesca laughed at her ability to so easily reminisce as of late. As she drove into the access for Cummington Street, she thought of how great it had been to speak with a handful of Athena graduates these past few days, despite the circumstances that had prompted such communications. To her, the women were more than friends. They were more than school buddies. They were her family.

Locating the parking lot just off Granby she had

found with the help of an online mapping Web site, Chesca parked in the best place to get to the Math-Computer Science building.

When she got out of the candy-apple-red Ford Edge, she took a moment to smooth down its nearly metallic exterior, as though it were her own prized possession, but Chesca's attention was soon diverted. To the southeast of campus, on the opposite side of the Massachusetts Turnpike, was the legendary Fenway Park. Though she had never been to a game, Chesca recognized its iconic status in proving that sometimes the underdog could indeed come out on top.

With spring training wrapped up and games starting, she could sense the smell of ballpark franks in the air as she waited for traffic to slow and a crosswalk to give the go-ahead for her to cross Commonwealth. Then, she walked along the pathway to the corner of Hinsdale and Cummington and took in the sights around her.

Being on campus almost made her wish she were back in school again, but that moment of nostalgia quickly disappeared as she remembered the all-night cramming sessions, bad cafeteria food and essay upon essay year after year.

Making the entrance into her location, Chesca quickly found the office and was pleasantly greeted with a smile.

"Miss Thorne?" the receptionist asked, upon Chesca's entrance.

The large, ornate grandfather clock informed her she

was right on time for her appointment, and she was grateful she hadn't dilly-dallied too much down memory lane. Just one stop would have Chesca late for her meeting with the head of the Computer Science department.

She nodded in affirmation, then the neatly dressed woman said, "This way please," and Chesca followed her through a bookcase-lined hallway to the corner office, which smelled of aged wood.

Though the department wasn't nearly as old as the rest of the campus, its furnishings were consistent with aged academia, creating a sense of immediate respect within Chesca, as though she had just entered the quiet calm of a historic library.

The receptionist tapped on the door as she opened it and escorted Chesca through as she announced, "Mr. Brighton, your eleven o'clock, sir."

"Have a seat, Miss..."

"Thorne. Francesca Thorne. Thank you for seeing me," she said, holding out a firm hand.

She took a seat directly across from his finely crafted desk, polished to an immaculate shine. Though it was hard not to peer around at her surroundings, taking in all that his office showed of his personality, Chesca concentrated on the middle-aged man in front of her as he spoke.

"I'm not sure I can help you with your request, Miss Thorne. From what you said over the phone, you're talking about a student who may have attended BU some time ago, if at all."

His salt-and-pepper hair was close-cut, though evidently slicked with some sort of gloss, its highlights lighting up under the glow of his desk lamp, as he rocked back and forth in the aged leather chair.

"This person—woman—would have been memorable, Mr. Brighton. As I briefly mentioned, she would have possessed incredible computer skills, enough for her to be recruited by the CIA. I'm certain she would have exhibited other traits," she said, hoping to imply more than her words said, "that such an organization would have found…useful."

The department head nodded along, as though he understood every word Chesca said, but she could tell he was still having some trouble piecing it together.

The fact of the matter was, this college student would have had to possess a great deal more than computer savvy to be attractive to the CIA.

Granted, at that time computers weren't as prevalent as they were today and someone knowing the inner workings of how to use and manipulate a variety of systems would have, indeed, presented a nice package to the government.

"I will add," she continued, "that this woman is suspected of being quite a dealer in blackmail, and as such she may have developed that talent years ago."

"Ah, well. I have only been the department head going on about twenty-five years, so thankfully I never experienced anything like that myself," he said.

Taking his time with his words, Mr. Brighton clearly was thinking of something more than what he was saying. Francesca would simply have to wait for his thoughts to come to fruition and give her an indication of whether or not she had reached a dead end.

"I might like to mention," he said after some time had passed between them. "It was quite odd for my predecessor to leave when he did. By policy, he had another decade left in him. Yet, something caused him to leave the academic world early, though I'm not certain if it is even relevant."

Though she had not mentioned her professional affiliation, and didn't feel it necessary to do so even now, Chesca made sure that when she twisted in her seated position, the inner pocket of her jacket flashed just the edge of her FBI badge. "Would you be able to point me in his direction?"

"I'll have my secretary give you his address," he said, as she suspected he would.

Mr. Brighton need not know whether or not this was official bureau business, and without her explaining it further, she suspected he wouldn't voluntarily open up that discussion himself. Sometimes, Chesca knew, it was the unsaid that got things done, more so than the use of words.

"Thank you, Mr. Brighton. I understand your predecessor would have left well after this woman was gone from campus, if she were ever here at all, but it's worth looking into."

As he got up to shake her hand, once again offering his slightly callused but warm palm, he nodded.

"I suppose he'll tell you himself, if he sees reason to,

so there's no harm in me mentioning this." His tone captivated Chesca and she made sure to drown out the sound of a nearby photocopier rallying to distract her senses with its repetitive output of paper. "Those last years he put in were indeed a struggle for him. Believe me, I worked day and night beside him, being mentored along the way. Something within him had changed. Whatever it was, it was eating at him long before he decided to call it quits."

Through his forced smile, Chesca could see pain, maybe even regret. "Thank you for telling me, Mr. Brighton. As you've said, he'll likely bring that up himself if it's relevant."

Not yet letting go of her hand, the slightly robust man, equal in her height, made sure to meet Chesca's eyes.

"Do understand, Miss Thorne, I respect that man. He never so much as hinted at any personal problems he may have experienced, and I never asked. I would prefer if you do not mention this little conversation we have had."

"Certainly, sir. Not to worry."

Following his lead out of the office and down the hallway back to the reception area, Chesca caught the scent of something earthy percolating. The receptionist was preparing a tea set complete with cookies and fruit.

"Give Miss Thorne the contact information for Mr. Schneider," Brighton instructed of his attentive receptionist, then added, "I'll take my tea now."

Knowing that was her cue to receive the information quickly and make her way out of the office, Chesca respectfully thanked each of them for their time and made a polite exit so that Brighton could get on with his evidently important and likely ritualistic tea service.

As she crossed Commonwealth Avenue to head back to the parking lot off Granby, Chesca momentarily checked her watch. She had been less than an hour with Brighton. Not bad. With the majority of the day left to her disposal she would be able to get a number of leads taken care of, and hopefully make some diligent progress on her assignment.

Or so she thought.

Chesca slowed her steps when she approached the rental car.

She could hardly believe it, given the short amount of time she had spent in the campus building.

From her stance directly in front of the car, it was clear someone had keyed the body on each side. Lines tracing the length of the automobile were etched deeply into the no longer fresh red paint.

When she noticed the tires were also gashed and flattened, she scooted down to the pavement and checked the undercarriage for anything to suggest further foul play.

Satisfied, but with more damage than she would have liked to have seen, Chesca let out a heavy sigh. Her day would evidently not be as cut-and-dried as she had hoped.

Now, added to her tasks, she would have to replace the rental car—and apologize profusely to the company, though fortunately she had insured the car against such predicaments—and due to the nature of the damage, it seemed Chesca would also be making a friendly stop at the local police precinct.

Once the quick and necessary phone calls were made to each, Chesca took a moment to sit on a concrete parking slab and rest her head in her hands, digging her elbows into her lap.

As she sat there, letting her temper at this inconvenience subside, she allowed a few moments to pass before she was able to admit the inevitable.

This was no coincidence.

It was not random.

Someone was trying to send a message.

As she carefully scanned the area, taking note of the passersby and being on the lookout for anything suspicious, Chesca hated the sinking feeling in her gut.

Despite only getting started, she knew without a doubt she couldn't hide this bit of information from Delphi. She would have to disclose what had happened, seeing how she had been warned more than once of the sensitivity of this case and the potential for risk.

Bethany had done her part in advising Chesca to watch her back, and now Chesca knew it was something she needed to seriously keep in mind. Those who had secrets to keep would do just about anything to keep them.

While Chesca was handy with a pistol and trained in martial arts, she wasn't cocky enough to assume she could handle anything and everything without at least clueing in her counterparts. It was her responsibility to Oracle to keep the agency abreast of how the case was going, whether there was reason to be alarmed or not.

Knowing her commitment to the case, Chesca sent a quick text message to Delphi informing her of the incident. She hoped to goodness it didn't come off as too quick for a mishap to happen, that something like this wouldn't have happened to someone else. But Chesca shook her head, reminding herself no matter who was on this case, if someone wanted to shut it down, they wouldn't be picky about their target.

It was rare for Chesca to get a call back on her cell phone, but within minutes Delphi was on the line. "You may want to consider finding another place to stay," the enigmatic voice said, no doubt using a disposable and untraceable mobile. "Double-check the hotel, but not until you have backup."

"Backup?" Chesca echoed, thinking she hadn't meant to come off as so needy.

With the nature of her job being mostly mental, Chesca had become accustomed to working on her own for the majority of a case, especially during the legwork. Only when she was out on the prowl for a suspect would she have someone tag along with her.

Then, as she thought about it, reflecting on all that she had learned about Giambi, Arachne and the Queen of Hearts personae, Chesca knew she had to swallow her pride. She was, in fact, working on a case that had already seen enough violence and danger in recent months, and she knew when to give in and just follow orders.

"No arguing. In the meantime," Delphi said, "keep me posted as to any other updates, so I can make sure to send the courier to the right place at a good time, okay?"

"Not a problem. May I ask, though, who this backup will be?"

"I wouldn't worry about it just yet," Delphi said. "What are your plans now? What's your destination?"

Chesca thought about it.

By the time the car company sent a representative to take care of this and exchange her car, and the police showed up to take a report, Chesca would be losing some much needed time. But she knew there was one thing she could handle without a babysitter.

"I'll be speaking with Schneider. Brighton gave me a lead on his predecessor in computer sciences," Chesca said, giving Delphi his address. "Then I'll be making a stop to chat with the local cops, if that makes sense to you."

Delphi agreed. "That should finish off your day. You'll have your partner by tomorrow. You have any idea where you'll be staying tonight?"

Chesca gritted her teeth.

She didn't want to argue with Delphi. As per her request, she wouldn't be returning to the hotel room until she could clear it with the assistance of whoever Oracle would be sending her way. And there was little point in checking into another hotel if the risk would be just about the same in Delphi's eyes.

She hated the idea of it.

It made her skin itch.

But what choice did she have?

"Yeah," Chesca said, grudgingly, before sharing the all-too-familiar address. Though she wasn't looking forward to the unplanned visit, Chesca knew one place with more security than Fort Knox to its credit. It would be the safest location for the short term. "I'll be staying with my parents."

Chapter 5

She should have known there was no way to avoid the inevitable.

Despite ignoring a serious handful of recent messages from her mother, Chesca kept trying to convince herself she didn't return the calls simply due to her busy nature at work, being assigned to the case in Baton Rouge, this, that...and just about every excuse in the book.

They were all excuses. She was just trying to avoid the same old conversation.

Though now that she was in her hometown, and clearly in need of a safe place to stay, there was no use in pretending she could get around a family visit. Sad that a forced opportunity had to be created to bring her back in touch with the Thorne mansion.

If Chesca had it her way, there would have been an abundance of reasons she would want to revisit her youthful home. But, sometimes life didn't work out how we wanted.

"I have been leaving you message after message, young lady. The least you could have done was let me know you were all right and not lying dead somewhere in the street." The stern voice of Abigail Thorne was coated in the same superficial sweetness Chesca had come to know as a child.

Even when being scorned by her mother's words, the actual tone came off as welcoming praise. The words "I am very disappointed in you" could have easily been exchanged with "this pâté de foie gras is positively sinful" on more than one occasion. It was an effect of her mother's Chesca had come to loathe, but expect.

No matter if she was being disciplined or praised, neither parent in the Thorne family fluctuated their tone with emotion. *It wasn't their way,* her mother would say, as though that was something to be proud of.

While Chesca said, "I was on a case, Mother. I'm calling you now, aren't I?" She double-checked the address Brighton had given her. She had found the location easily enough, with her memory never fully removed from the familiarity of her hometown landscape.

The rental car had been substituted within thirty minutes, which pleased Chesca. She didn't quite know what to expect, or how the company would take it considering the condition of the car she was trading back to them. Luckily, they were accommodating, swift with courteous service, and shrugged off the incident as all in a day's work.

The street cops who checked out the damaged rental were just as quick. A simple report was all that was needed, and anything further Chesca wanted to inquire about would be best handled at the precinct, so overall she lost very little time in her day after such an inconvenience.

She had to keep reminding herself that hers was not the first car that had been tampered with in the history of Athena women digging into the mystery of Arachne. And it likely wouldn't be the last.

"Never mind that, Francesca. I'm terribly disappointed," her mother carried on. "You missed the brunch I hosted for the foundation stewards. Though I wonder if it is too much to ask that you do not miss the annual gala?"

Chesca let out a groan, wanting to kick herself for not remembering. Along with extra sunshine, April brought the annual Thorne Family Foundation fund-raising gala. She should have known she'd be the recipient of a not-so-gentle reminder of the upcoming event.

It was a pet project of Abigail's, touted to support whichever newsworthy charity struck her short-lived interest.

Each year there was somehow a more tragic or endearing cause the foundation rallied for, though the lack of sincerity behind the project always left Chesca feeling disenchanted. She knew it was just an excuse for her mother to host pretentious social gatherings and wave around her clout amongst fellow blue bloods.

She also knew she had an unspoken responsibility to attend at least two events per year, representing the next generation of Thornes. Unspoken, but never forgotten in the eyes of her parents.

Francesca had been a disappointment to socialites Abigail and Dorian. Her parents were of discerning blood, she was often told, who had risen to a certain status amongst their well-to-do crowd. It simply wasn't anything Chesca wanted to be a part of. And the notion that she wouldn't be carrying on some of the most well-established family traditions was interpreted as a slap in the face, especially to her father.

It was no secret her parents had hoped for a male child, someone to be a proper heir to the family legacies and leave a healthy dose of offspring as namesakes. Unwilling to be matched up using the sole criteria of money, Chesca simply didn't know how to play by the family rules.

Once her parents accepted this fact, however, they made it quite simple for everyone to get along. Francesca was to put on her party face at least twice annually, to pay respects to the community as part of the Thorne family, and in return she would have her pick of extracurricular activities and academics to choose from.

Though graduating long ago, and no longer feeling the least bit dependent on her family for anything,

Chesca knew that deal had a never-ending clause. One that she thought was fair to keep, for the most part.

After all, it was her family and their connections that had contributed to Chesca's desires as a young girl. Allowing her to be involved in activities that likely contributed to her attracting the attention of the Athena Academy. And, with that potential connection to her success,. Chesca reminded herself often to bite her tongue, and play the role of dutiful daughter.

"I asked if you will be attending the annual gala, Francesca. You will make it, won't you?"

She couldn't come up with a fast enough reason not to. She was in Boston, she would be staying at the family home. What could she possibly have to say that would convince her mother she couldn't attend? She was never good at hiding things from her mother, that was for sure.

It was as though she was once again a schoolgirl, being challenged by her mother's intolerance for secrets.

The one time Chesca had received a childhood love note from a classmate, she did everything in her power to shield it from her mother's all-knowing senses. When it was found by a housekeeper under her canopy bed, Chesca tried to deny knowing of its existence until it was rattled out of her by Abigail Thorne's ability to stare down her sole offspring and demand a confession. This, of course, was followed by a lecture on how it was inappropriate for an eight-year-old girl to be carrying on with a boy one year her senior.

The memory caused Chesca to chuckle in embarrassment, and knowing she would face inevitable defeat, she told her mother, "Yes, that sounds fine. Thank you for the invitation."

There was silence on the other end of the phone.

"Mother?"

There was a clearing of her throat, then Abigail spoke softly. "Why, might I ask, are you so agreeable? Usually, I am forced to ask you at least three times before you agree to attend such an event. Is something wrong?"

Francesca didn't know whether to laugh or roll her eyes, so she did both. Leave it to her mother to be overly dramatic.

"No, everything's fine. However, I do have to ask a favor," Chesca began amidst the almost immediate protests of her mother. "But I'm sure it's a favor you'll appreciate."

When her mother finally stopped protesting, Chesca was able to inform her of her whereabouts and request permission to stay at the house until further notice.

"Francesca! We'd love to have you here," her mother cooed with a quiet pride that still seemed tinged with a lack of authenticity. "Quite honestly, it would be fabulous to have you assist with the final plans for the gala. Perhaps you could—"

"I'm afraid not," Chesca interrupted. "I am here for a work assignment, Mother. While I am happy to attend, and if there are any small tasks I can tend to while at the reception, I'd be happy to help, please keep in mind the purpose of me being in Boston is work. That has to come first."

"Doesn't it always," her mother said, almost sounding defeated. "Of course, dear. As you wish."

Feeling a tad bit guilty about getting her mother's hopes up, she did her best to smooth things over as she gave a time estimate of when the family could expect her. Because of their rocky relationship, Chesca had a hard time believing her mother would truly want to spend quality one-on-one time with her.

Wrapping up what should have been a very quick call, Chesca was bittersweet when she finally hung up. She felt both relieved to have gotten the conversation over with, but also anxious about her forthcoming stay at the Thorne residence.

However, there were more pressing issues on her mind, and she knew all too well she'd have plenty of time to contemplate the ins and outs of being a Thorne family member later, apparently over this evening's dinner.

For now, Chesca's sights were set on the narrow brownstone-style home across the street. This was, apparently, where she would find Schneider, and she took in a deep breath as she made her way to the doorbell to signal her arrival.

The front landing was decorated with bright spring flowers, indicative of someone's passion for artful presentation. While the home itself had faded in its years, it had an old-world charm about it that made Chesca fond of its appearance. It looked well loved, despite its obvious age.

"May I help you?" an older woman asked, catching Chesca off guard. She hadn't even knocked or rung the bell yet, having been so caught up in the beauty of this home's facade.

She offered a smile and in as pleasant a voice as possible—she didn't want to make the matter seem too pressing—Chesca requested to see Mr. Schneider. "I was referred to him by an old colleague of his at the university."

"Really," the stately woman said in more of an accusation than a question. "And who might that have been?"

She desired to uphold the promise made to Brighton that she would not divulge what he had shared of his predecessor, but she saw no harm in doing a little bit of name-dropping if it would get her in the front door.

"Mr. Brighton."

There was a brief moment of what appeared to be silence, then from somewhere down the hall, Chesca heard a mumble, followed by the newly warmed vocal pitch of the woman at the door. "Won't you please come in, Miss—"

"Thorne. Francesca Thorne," she said, extending her hand to meet her host and following the woman inside the dimly lit hallway.

With overpowering reds and purples, the paintings and wall hangings covered the pale, yellowed paint of years gone by. Her eyes adjusted as Chesca trailed the woman to an open room, introduced through French doors that were in dire need of a paint job. The interior gave off a musty, stuffy scent, despite the bowls of potpourri and fresh flowers decorating the room.

"Mr. Schneider, this is your guest, Miss Francesca Thorne. Shall I bring in some coffee for the two of you?"

Chesca was about to protest the unnecessary gesture, but Schneider nodded his head, and motioned for Chesca to sit across from him on a velvet, and terribly uncomfortable, wing-back chair.

The aged man, hunched at the back and appearing stiff in his propped-up position against a leather recliner that clearly wasn't meant for reclining, Schneider puffed on a manly pipe. He obligingly asked, "Do you mind?" but evidently didn't wait for, nor want, an answer.

She shook her head and got straight to the point. Chesca was eager to hear why the man had left his post earlier than others had anticipated, and she desperately wanted to hear of any connection to her suspect.

"I understand you were the head of the computer sciences department prior to Brighton."

"Indeed," he said, though Chesca had to lean forward to properly hear him, his voice was low and gruff, the pipe masking his intonation. Chesca wondered if this was deliberate.

"I wonder, sir, if you may be of assistance to me then," Chesca began, and offered the basic rundown of the person she was hunting. "As I've mentioned, this woman would have been quite crafty with computers, but more so with the art of manipulation. There would have been something unique about her skills and perhaps her social demeanor that the CIA would have found appealing."

Francesca watched as Schneider puffed away on his pipe, seemingly drifting off at times into her words, or perhaps tracking his memory to a point in time he could recall with clarity.

"Do you take cream or sugar?"

The question unfortunately interrupted her analysis of the elderly man. She wanted to pay careful attention to his thought processes, watch him as he formulated long-lost memories in his present-day mind, be watchful of any movements or tics that would indicate his attempts at fictionalizing truths.

"Black. Please, and thank you," Chesca said, accepting the cup of fine bone china. Definitely a contrast to the takeout cups she was used to on a daily basis.

Though she accepted the beverage as gracefully as she could, she never once took her eyes off her current informant.

She imagined this would be what a bookish grandfather would look like, though she had no familial comparison to consider. Her grandparents were long ago deceased, when Chesca was too young to remember much of anything about them.

But Schneider's disposition, his mannerisms, his calm and still posture had *academic* written all over it.

Chesca imagined how his mornings were likely spent studying the daily newspapers, how his afternoon naps were followed by reading nonfiction, likely history or war biographies, and then his short hours after dinner were simply spent contemplating the day.

Well, at least that's how Chesca romanticized and imagined his time to be like. Of course, with his quiet nature and shortness of words, she supposed she might not be all that far off. Especially with the stacks of loose papers and books set around the room. It almost appeared as if Schneider were still coming home to grade papers every night.

"There was a time," he said, slowly and deliberately, as though his memory had just caught up with him and he didn't like it.

Francesca studied his facial expression as he spoke, his eyes staring across the room to the unlit fireplace, as though that were a safe place to focus as he reflected on his past.

"There was a time I had a lady friend," he drawled, "when I was employed by the university. 'Course, back then, such things were not made as public as they are now."

Allowing him to focus on his storytelling, Chesca sat back in her chair as best as possible. To appear comfortable as she listened to his slow speech, she decided to enjoy the mild roast blend of coffee she had been served. Evidently, Schneider would not give her the satisfaction of a short version.

He amused himself with recounting policies and protocol for staff and instructors at the university, of how entertaining members of the opposite sex was considered taboo, when they were either employed by, educated by, or even remotely associated with the campus. Of course, he also explained how common it was for such rules to be broken. Apparently, nothing much had changed on campus.

"She was stunning," he continued, but with bitterness in his tone and an empty stare in his eyes. The way he said it, it almost seemed vindictive, and Chesca was careful to watch every word he spoke for further information. "And very smart."

"With computers?" Chesca asked, after the man had taken more than a few beats of silence.

"More than that, I'm afraid." He cleared his throat a couple of seconds, sounding like a lawn-mower engine that had run out of gas. "Smart at getting her way. Getting what she wanted."

For a moment, Schneider continued to stare at the vacant fireplace, but his eyes eventually moved over to meet Chesca's, as he gave her a knowing look. "She was resourceful."

Giving him a moment to reflect and absorb his memories, Chesca wondered when would be too soon to interrupt and ask for an identity. She wanted desperately to know who this woman was, where she could find her, how she'd gone from being an academically excellent youth to a worldwide conspirator.

"How so, Mr. Schneider? What was your experience with her?"

The shadowed figure at the door alarmed Chesca,

until she recognized the woman who'd answered the door peering around the corner. "Is everything all right in here, sir?" she asked, and Chesca knew she wasn't asking about the coffee.

"Fine, go on," he said, shooing her off. "I'm telling my story. I'm telling it the way it was."

The air in the room began to feel heavy, thick almost, with the tension this topic brought into the atmosphere. Clearly, this was something Schneider had been keeping to himself for some time and it was an effort for him to share it.

Why he had chosen to share it with Francesca was unknown to her, but she knew well enough that those with histories worth sharing often did so in their own time.

"She double-crossed me in time," he finally said, steering the conversation right where Chesca wanted to go. "Made sure I was good and hooked, left me with no alternative, and then stabbed me in the back. She was a wretched woman. Of course, she hid that well from me in the beginning. No wonder the CIA recruited her. She was no ordinary student."

He carried on in a bitter tone, revealing how he had struck up an off-campus relationship with a student who excelled in everything, including the art of manipulation, and how he'd allowed himself to get in deep enough to be blackmailed.

Chesca knew this was her ticket to finding out something real about the CIA recruit. She could barely sit still in her eagerness to hear more.

"Waved my career in front of my nose, like fly bait, and gave me an ultimatum. I had to leave my position, you see. There was too much at risk. I don't mind making a fool of myself, evidently, but I wasn't willing to embarrass my school. I no longer carry the shame I once did," the man said, nodding his head in agreement with himself. "Thus I don't mind telling you so much. I trust," he said, nodding toward the FBI identification that could barely be seen against Chesca's trousers, "this is important information to you."

"It is, sir. I appreciate your candor," Chesca said, allowing the man to continue his confession.

"In that case, I hope you find Jackie and do with her what you must."

"Jackie?"

"Jackie Cavanaugh," he said, with a slightly pleasant tone in his voice. "I'm sure you don't need me to introduce you to that family."

"No, sir, you don't," Chesca said, letting that information sink in for a moment. "Thank you for your time. I'm sorry to hear the university lost a man such as yourself prematurely. Though I wish you the best, and am truly grateful for your time. And the coffee."

The stout woman walked Chesca out the door. She stood still on the side of the narrow side street where Schneider lived, and looked back at the brownstone. She couldn't believe what information he had shared with her.

Jackie Cavanaugh.

No, the Cavanaugh family needed no introduction.

For any local the Cavanaughs were a name you didn't easily forget.

Everyone liked to stay clear of the Mafia.

Chapter 6

Now knowing what she did about who she was seeking, Chesca made an appointment with a detective from the Major Crimes unit at police headquarters. Why head off for a precinct when she could potentially reel in much juicier information from the powers that be?

Unable to get in for a briefing the same day, however, due to the lateness of the afternoon, Chesca settled on a meeting the next day. She didn't like putting off that important step to gaining local insight, but she also knew her time would be well spent sharing her findings with her Oracle contact.

If Delphi was working on gathering CIA information to send along to Chesca, a name from all those years ago would be beneficial in digging up the past.

Not wanting to divulge that amount of information over the phone, Chesca settled into the notion that an e-mail update might be best. She would be able to outline her accomplishments, share the news flash of the Mafia connection, and have a document she could refer back to, as secondary notes.

In order to do that, however, Chesca needed to plug in her laptop and she neither had the desire to do so on the side of the road, nor at a coffee shop. She needed space and comfort, privacy and quiet. And that meant it was time.

Making the drive to her childhood home as pleasant as possible under the circumstances, Chesca opted for a short cut she knew, which also happened to offer breathtaking views of the waterfront.

If there was one thing about home she did miss, it was the smell of salty air, the slight waft of seafood being served at one of the many five-star restaurants they'd frequented, and the simplicity and beauty a gorgeous waterscape could offer.

Though she rarely spent time enjoying the shores and sunshine in a truly youthful way—bikini-clad and flirting with boys as other girls did—Chesca did have a fondness for the water, and was thankful to have been out on a few watercrafts in her younger days. The Thorne family did a lot of entertaining, and that didn't stop at the water's edge. Quite frequently, during those warm summer months, Abigail and Dorian were elite guests at some moneybags's yacht party or cruise line celebration disguised as a philanthropic event.

Despite being too young to truly participate in the facade, as the daughter of two prominent parents, Chesca was often towed along to make sure everyone knew what a fine job the Thornes had done raising their purebred daughter.

It was a mockery, feeling like prodded cattle, Chesca recalled. Whatever it took to put on a good public face. But no one had a say in the family hand they were dealt, and Chesca was no exception. She knew better than to take her well-funded life for granted, but it was still disturbing how unnecessary it seemed to show off quite so much as her parents and their social circle did.

Even from a young age, her mother had trained and primped her, holding out hope Francesca would turn into the belle of the ball, delight and attract fellow blue bloods, and land herself a happily ever after matched up with some suitable, and well-pocketed, name. But that was never Chesca's desire.

After seeing what falsities existed in that social circle, and the damage it had done to an already superficial marriage between her parents, Chesca vowed she would never entertain marriage for the sake of appearances. If anything, she would marry for love.

She knew it was a concept her parents couldn't relate to. But to her, the amount of energy a person could put into something that wasn't even real never did make sense.

That was something she encountered on a regular

basis, however, especially in her chosen field. Chesca found it often took more energy for criminals to keep up their chosen lives, and they usually received less financial rewards, than had they just chosen to lead a productive life.

She knew it wasn't as simple as that. There was more at work in the criminal mind than just trying to make a quick buck. More often than not, there were personal vendettas, scores to settle and a bewildering sense of entitlement propelling such actions.

As an undergrad, Chesca's time had been spent studying human behavior and criminal psychology. One year in particular, Chesca was listening to a three-hour speech on a warped cassette tape, preparing for a lengthy presentation she needed to make for her class. The memorable speech was given by Theodore M. Hesburgh, and the one thing that really stuck in her memory was how a few simple words could emphasize such a large point. Hesburgh had commented on how easy it was to be virtuous at a distance. It was such a simple observatory concept, yet so true that Chesca considered it in everything she worked on.

She knew how easily a criminal mind could con someone into essentially handing over well-earned money. How disguises were not always physical, and a few well-crafted words could woo the weak. This one simple, uncomplicated quote, remembered from her studies, was true in all of what Chesca had witnessed over the years.

She was raised in such an environment, after all. The

Thorne family presented the picture-perfect portrait of what a family ought to be, but behind the scenes it was anything but perfect. Both her mother and father carried on not-so-secretive affairs. They barely conversed with one another when not in the public eye.

And despite seeming proud of their daughter when bragging to some other parent in their social group, Chesca knew it was no secret her parents were incredibly disappointed in the life she chose to lead.

And now, as a highly regarded forensic psychologist for the Federal Bureau of Investigation, the Hesburgh quote was a tidy reminder to Chesca that people are not always what they seem to be, and a good facade could mask just about anything.

This was never more true, she was learning, than in her current task of profiling the powerful blackmailer known as Arachne. With a vengeful streak against the one thing Chesca knew she could truly trust—the Athena Academy for the Advancement of Women—Arachne had been doing whatever it took to get her message across.

Multiple personalities, lifelong aliases and disguises?

Seems like a sociopath to me, Chesca thought to herself.

As she rounded her way onto the last scenic stretch, traveling back to her family roots, Chesca did her best to balance the wheel as she set down her takeout coffee cup, making a hand available for answering an incoming call.

"Miss Thorne," the voice said when she answered. Though she couldn't quite pinpoint it, she knew it was distantly familiar. She'd heard the calm but dignified pitch before, though she couldn't trace it in her mind quick enough to satisfy her curiosity.

The caller ID was no help, with the label of unknown caller.

But as the voice on the opposite end of the line announced pleasantly, "This is Christine Evans," Chesca felt her face light up. She was surprised to hear from the Athena Academy principal and longtime academic developer recruited by Marion Gracelyn.

"It's a pleasure," Chesca said, balancing her attention between the honored phone call and the winding road leading to the exclusive landscaped gardens of her parent's home.

Christine Evans had a long history with Marion Gracelyn, having crossed paths before the Academy was even started. Though she was victim to an accident that caused the loss of her vision, Christine was one who could see through anyone, cut to the chase, and offer introspective perceptions on all the interesting characters Chesca had come to know and love at the Academy. With her skillful background, Christine assisted at the birth of the school, developing the academic and physical training modules, and it became her passion to carry on the dream she shared with Marion Gracelyn, to make Athena Academy something extraordinary.

Chesca had, on more than one occasion, had the pleasure of conversation with this woman, and hearing her voice now was both a surprising gift, and a reason to be very curious as to the intent of the call.

"You remember my great-nephew William?" Christine asked, taking up the conversation as though it hadn't been years since they'd last spoken. "The son of my brother's son, who was an occasional visitor to the Academy when I needed an extra set of strong hands?"

Though her recollection of William was rough, Chesca knew she had seen him once or twice around the grounds. It had been a long time since her younger days, and her memory was fuzzy. "Somewhat," she said, not wanting to offend one of her mentors in not vividly remembering someone who was obviously dear to her.

"Then you'll recognize him," Christine said, as though it were a matter of fact.

Before she tempered her surprise, Chesca blurted out a quick, "Excuse me?"

Despite the distance over the phone, she swore she could detect a smile in Christine's voice. "I have it on good authority you're working on something of particular interest to the Academy, and have unfortunately run into some troubles."

"Yes, but—" she began to protest, not wanting Christine to worry that she was having troubles on the case. Then she realized it was rude of her to interrupt. "Pardon me. Yes, there was an incident."

"I've instructed William to accompany your crusade from now on. For the duration of your assignment, at any rate."

Christine gathered information from Chesca on how and where William could find her, and she offered up additional insight into her great-nephew's strengths. "He's quite the bodyguard. Had been with the U.S. Army for some time now, but unfortunately took a bullet recently."

For a moment, Chesca cringed, wondering how helpful a wounded partner would be. Did she risk the possibility that he would only slow her down? Christine, however, quietly reassured her that her kin would be an advantage to Chesca's pursuit.

"Don't let that fool you," she said. "He may have just come off the wounded list, but no bullet will keep him grounded. Will's been up to nothing but his usual tricks, taking advantage of his time off to hunt and fish. It'll do him well to put his mind to work and accompany you with your quest."

Being an analytical introvert who preferred to work solo, Chesca was hesitant about having someone tag along with her on her efforts. It was somewhat frustrating and annoying that she needed backup so early on, as Delphi suggested, and she didn't need a bodyguard who wasn't in top form.

Yet she knew it was an honor to be considered by Oracle for this assignment, and if both Delphi and the respected Christine Evans believed it in her best interest to have company for her task, she knew it was unwise to argue.

As an Oracle agent, Chesca had learned it was best not to ask questions. So despite her mild resentment of having been assigned a partner, she knew she would abide by the command, and try to make the best of the situation.

"Thank you," Chesca offered, idling the car alongside a single lane road, wanting to pay full attention to her conversation with the Academy principal before continuing her route home. "I appreciate your concern, and William sounds like he'll be a welcome addition to my case."

She cringed as she said this, wondering if she had inherited the ability to bullshit from her Thorne family upbringing. In all honesty, she hoped she came off as sincere. It would simply take a while to warm up to the idea of working with a partner.

"Do keep in touch, and let me know if I can be of further assistance," Christine offered, before saying her goodbye.

Before picking up where she left off on the road to the Thorne house, Chesca allowed herself to soak in all that had happened since her arrival in Boston. Her to-do list was ever increasing, and now she had the task of putting aside some pride and welcoming Will Evans to her side.

Perhaps they could divide and conquer, Chesca thought. She did want to get a few integral things covered over the next twenty-four hours, so perhaps by dividing up the tasks and sending Will off to… No. That wouldn't work.

She accepted Christine's offer to have Will accompany her, and had agreed with Delphi's suggestion that she have an additional body on her side as she set out to profile Arachne. She couldn't go back on her word.

Besides, Chesca thought, it was simply a matter of time before she could offer up some intel to Oracle and call this case closed. How bad could it be to have to share the task with someone?

Chesca knew Christine Evans was a pleasant individual with an intriguing personality. If she so fondly thought of her great-nephew, knowing Chesca well enough to understand her style and skills, she must have presumed on some level the two of them would be a compatible match for this assignment.

Between her appointment with the Major Crimes unit and wanting to follow up on the information provided by Schneider, Chesca had more than a day's work planned for the next twenty-four hours. But before that, there was one thing Chesca needed to take care of, so that she could hurry up and get settled in, and share her findings of the day with Delphi.

It was one small step, but she could feel her feet dragging when she finally got the nerve to pull into the Thorne driveway.

With her bare necessities in hand, only the few spare items she wasn't forced to abandon at the hotel room, Chesca walked up the cobblestone steps to the grand entrance of the Thorne mansion.

The simple act of breathing in the air, letting her mind wrap around scent memories related to her younger years spent in this overly large homestead, Chesca took in a sigh and prepared for the worst, but hoped for the best.

Once inside the foyer, Chesca was greeted by her mother's disapproving frown. "You've gained weight."

Letting a chuckle roll off her emotions, Chesca did the best she could in presenting a respectable smile.

"Nice to see you too, Mother."

Chapter 7

"Dinner will be served at seven," Abigail said, her eyes roaming across her daughter's physique.

Had she gained weight? Possibly.

It had been several months since Chesca had seen her mother, right around the time of the holidays just passed, so her mother could have easily noticed any slight fluctuation. But Chesca was never one to track pound by pound her size and shape, knowing full well she was in top form due to the rigorous physical training she voluntarily participated in to maintain her strength, stamina and defensive skills.

But to Abigail Thorne, five pounds in any direction implied an atrocity worthy of shame, something to work at removing as a fault within one's character. Attempting to defend her well-toned and active body as a source of pride, however, would do no good for Chesca.

She was a healthy weight, an average size for her five-foot-six-inch body. Her toned physique, thanks to regular Pilates, yoga and martial arts training was something Chesca worked hard to achieve.

Her body was a weapon, and she not only treated it right, she made sure to eat as healthily as possible even when on the go. Her only vice was the coffee she consumed when needing an extra kick of adrenaline, and even that she opted to take black, no sugar or cream, and thus had a hard time accepting that as a fault.

"I'm healthy. Isn't that what really matters?" Chesca said, dropping her few personal items on a finely crafted antique sideboard.

"Elaine Vermont's daughter Eloise is so thin these days," Abigail said, with as much pride as was to be expected by someone who valued personal appearances over health and well-being.

It was no secret that along with public pleasantries and handshakes, a teeny tiny shape was also coveted amongst the elite. Prim. Proper. Pale and petite. It was enough to make Chesca want to scarf down a double cheeseburger.

"I'd say good for her, but I doubt it is," she instead retorted, though she hoped to sway the conversation in another direction before her mother began the usual criticism of how unladylike it was for her to have any muscle whatsoever.

Chesca was proud of her body and what it was

capable of accomplishing. Just because she didn't fit into the ideal her mother laid out for her did not mean she was a lesser person. It had taken years to realize that on her own, having heard enough about her destined size and shape from her mother as a child, and what her expectations were for a Thorne family member.

In contrast, Chesca valued how different their opinions were on physical fitness and appearances. It was much more critical to Chesca that her body possess adequate muscle and stamina for those times she needed to exert herself physically while on a manhunt. Had she been the twig figure her mother desired her daughter to be, she'd never stand a chance at fighting off predators.

"Your room has been prepared for you," Abigail Thorne said, matter-of-factly, sounding annoyed that she didn't have more notice to prepare.

Within a heartbeat, after Chesca finally ventured off on her own as an adult, her mother had had the childhood bedroom completely renovated and redecorated, not one for being nostalgic. At the time, Chesca had felt like her mother rushed her out of the house, eager to have the opportunity to transform the room more to her old-world liking, replacing Chesca's preferences with stuffy textiles and uncomfortable furnishings.

The transformation had taken less than a week, and it was a dramatic contrast to the room Francesca had spent many nights in, quietly contemplating the world and her personal ambitions as an eager and adventurous young girl.

"Thank you," she said to her mother, collecting her belongings. "I have a bit of work to do right away, but it'll be nice to catch up during dinner."

Despite the knot in her stomach at the idea of spending the night under her parents' roof, Chesca at least wanted to offer some dignity and pleasantries, in respect to her family and in appreciation for letting her drop in on such short notice.

It was a slow ascent up the pristine polished stairwell, dark wood which beautifully reflected the lights from the chandelier above. Chesca took each step deliberately, feeling as though each step was one further from her life's reality and into the past. But this would be no walk down memory lane. She was here, in Boston, on business and she fully intended to keep it that way.

While it was her duty, her obligation, to participate in a handful of family functions, and she would extend the courtesy of attending the spring gala, Chesca was determined to make her stay a short one, focusing on the task at hand, and getting back to her own life in Richmond.

Though it was hard not to let the environment filter into her emotions. Everything from the décor to the smells to the general aura in this multigenerational home fed memories to Chesca, some which made her lips curl into a smile, and others she'd just as soon forget.

As she made the walk down the hall to the double doors leading into her old bedroom, Chesca wasn't immune to the reminder that she was raised well. She'd had anything and everything she wished for provided for her, and had no right to complain about her upbringing.

Yet it wasn't so easy to forget how much she'd yearned, as a young girl, to have the opportunity to have friends over—real friends, not the ones imposed upon her from her family's social circle—and have a normal, television-style childhood.

Chesca laughed.

She wondered if anyone was satisfied with their childhood or if it was just human nature to grumble on forever about things parents control and children do not.

When she entered the room, she felt assaulted with the abundance of pastels. It was as though her mother fashioned the room after a baby or bridal shower, light blues and pinks and a fair amount of lavender thrown in to make this feminine décor almost too much.

It was much more soft, in a deliberately elegant way, than Chesca would ever assume for herself. It was too frilly. Too fluffy. But it would serve the purpose in what she needed. A bed to crash on and a private room in which to work.

Once she got over the initial shock of how primly this room was laid out, Chesca laid out her things on the bed and took in an assessment of what she had in her possession. She would need to find some clothing for the next day. She was certain her mother would help in this regard, but for now she simply wanted to get back to working on the case. Her wardrobe could wait.

It took some time to wade through the tapestries and

textiles to find the appropriate place to plug in her laptop and get logged in to the working world, but Chesca soon had set up a makeshift home office that would do the trick just fine.

She immediately logged into her e-mail account to share her findings with Oracle. Sending a message to Delphi, Chesca outlined the information she learned from both Brighton and Schneider, about a female student who'd earned a quick reputation for manipulating computers and humans equally before being recruited by the CIA.

The most interesting news she had to share was the name provided by Schneider. Jackie Cavanaugh.

It was remarkable to learn that this woman, believed to be responsible for so much heartache and turmoil at Athena, could have had a head start in crime from a Mafia upbringing. It was definitely something Chesca would pursue further, and she hoped to find more details on this woman's past during her meeting with the Major Crimes unit the next day at police headquarters.

As it was, she already knew of the family, having come across their name through various criminal investigations. While she had never personally encountered any of them, or handled any cases pertaining to their underground finances and activities, she was aware of their reputation.

The differences in how some mob families operated and conducted business was interesting to Francesca. While there was hardly any way she could describe some as respectable, there was a stark contrast between those families that chose to operate in old-world dignity and those who claimed the streets as their own personal battlefield.

From what Chesca understood with her minimal personal knowledge of the Cavanaugh family, they were technically old news. The family heads had long since passed and the younger generation had merely turned into thugs and headed up street gangs. They were definitely not the sort to be romanticized in Mafia films.

This clan was much more gritty, destructive and careless to all those around them.

That was the part that worried her the most. Chesca had an odd respect for the intricacies of organized crime, but had no patience for stupid criminals or vindictive thugs. It was a personal perspective she was often mocked for, since in her line of work a criminal was just a criminal, no matter what they did or how they did it.

With her passion for forensic psychology, however, she knew there was a difference between those who operated family businesses and unfortunately chose to settle their own scores, and those families whose sole intent was to bring anyone and everyone down around them, no matter what the cost.

What Chesca was not previously aware of, however, was that there was potentially a connection between Arachne and a local Boston gang. It wasn't a stretch of the imagination that being brought up in a life of crime could lead one to conduct all sorts of atrocities, and it certainly put a new twist on her investigation. Who knows what connections this character could have that extended to other Mafias, other cities, other countries.

Chesca vowed to find out.

When her message to Delphi was complete, Chesca typed up some of her own personal notes, for follow-up and to keep track of what she wanted to check on in the coming day. She already had a few key questions in mind for the local law enforcement, and with whatever intel she could gather through Oracle, she felt as though she had her fair share of work cut out for her.

Chesca shook her head at how quickly things could change. Though she had no complaints. It was this very thing, the thrill of the hunt, the adrenaline rush, that she enjoyed so much in her line of work.

Some cases were more paperwork than actual investigation, and while it was nice to take a break from the streets from time to time, she truly felt at her best when she had her nose to the ground, sniffing out her prey. With so many different personality types and an endless supply of crime to investigate, Chesca was never bored with her profession, always working on something new. Thankfully that kept her mind fresh, active and eager to continue the daily grind.

She took a moment to send a follow-up e-mail to the team in Baton Rouge, informing them she was on the road for another case. Though her part in their case was complete, she wanted to ensure they knew how to reach her if they had anything for her to follow up on.

Plus, it was always a good idea to keep positive relationships with fellow agents and cops. The number of people she came into contact with and worked with, even for short durations of time, meant always needing someone for something. It was Chesca's motto to always leave a good impression and keep her face in the good books of colleagues.

Between the relationships she developed at the Athena Academy, and the professionals she came into contact with around the country through her position in the FBI, Francesca had a very impressive address book. Some were friends, some were purely professional connections, but she was grateful to know proficient and highly trained individuals who shared the same goals and ambitions she did: Getting the bad guy and finding some justice in this world.

While she read the confirmation from Delphi that the files had come through without a hitch, Chesca was startled from her working privacy as a tap at the door signaled the arrival of her mother.

"Dinner will be served in less than an hour, Francesca," she said, eyeing what she no doubt viewed as the mess Chesca was able to make in a very short time. "Is that what you'll be wearing?"

Holding back on her inner emotions of wanting to shoo off her mother's disapproval, Chesca thought for a moment before speaking and bit her tongue. "Yes. In fact, this is all I have to wear. No other choice, so I apologize for the informality."

Through her legwork carried on during the day, Chesca was comfortable but presentable in basic jeans, a black T-shirt, and a tailored blazer. It had been perfect for running around to the university campus and then following the lead to Schneider's house. How was she to know to keep extra clothing on hand in case she wouldn't be able to return to her hotel room for some fashionable wardrobe changes?

"Very well then. But I did notice," Abigail said, picking off a drooping petal from the abundant flower arrangement sitting on an antique dresser, "the lack of luggage upon your arrival. Considering the gala is tomorrow and you're no doubt prepared with some excuse about work being your priority, I've arranged an appointment for you with Roger. He'll meet you here, so I expect you to hold up the arrangement I have made with him."

Roger.

The mere mention of his name sent shivers down Chesca's spine. For as long as she could remember, her mother's personal shopper and stylist had practically been a part of the family, stopping in regularly to fashion the Thorne closets and update anything that was at risk of becoming "so last season."

He was more than eccentric. He was downright annoying.

The man acted as though it was a crime to wear anything off the rack, and thus he adored Abigail

Thorne who always insisted on having the so-called best of everything. Including ridiculously overpriced fashion imports.

It was all too much for the no-nonsense Chesca, but considering her lack of apparel, let alone her apparent need for something to wear to the obligatory family fund-raiser, she had little choice but to accept defeat.

"Fine. When is the appointment?"

Chesca watched as her mother tried hard to act as though she weren't being a busybody and letting her eyes roam across her daughter's belongings. Honestly, it was though she had never seen a laptop before.

All Chesca had to her credit was her working files, the computer, and her handbag—which, granted, had somehow spilled its disheveled contents out along the mattress when she tossed it there, carelessly. But there was nothing there worthy of her mother's horrific eye-rolling.

"Tomorrow morning. Nine o'clock."

Chesca shook her head. "That won't work. You'll have to call him to reschedule."

"I'll do no such thing. Roger is a very busy man, Francesca. He's in such high demand, and considering this is high season for social gatherings he's not the easiest man to get a hold of, you should know that. You're lucky he's even accommodating you for this last-minute appointment."

Flopping back onto the bed, feeling like a teenager who was protesting a hyperactive debate with an impatient parent, Chesca let out a sigh, wondering how to convince her mother it simply wouldn't work. There wouldn't be enough time.

She had an appointment set up at police headquarters. She didn't want to waste the morning and lose valuable time being fitted by an aggressive and opinionated fashion consultant. Why couldn't her mother understand she was here for work, and not to fall back into the role of puppet daughter?

"Mother, I have an appointment that I really cannot be late for. I'm here for work. The gala comes second. I'm sorry."

As the words came out of her mouth the tension in the room reached the point of breaking, and Chesca did her best to be patient in waiting for the next verbal punch from her mother.

"Perhaps Roger can come for eight or eight-thirty. But between getting the two of you properly suited for the gala and finding you something reasonable to wear while you're here, Roger won't have much time, you understand."

Chesca wasn't sure if she had simply misunderstood, or missed a point being made by her mother, so she asked for clarification. "Who's the two of us, Mother?"

"You and your friend. You don't expect him to wear jeans to the gala do you, or did you two plan this ahead?"

No doubt due to the dumbfounded look upon her daughter's face, Abigail Thorne carried on. "And don't think it's okay to invite guests here, Francesca, without at least having the courtesy to inform me so I can properly prepare."

Despite her mother's efforts, it took a moment for Chesca to think of to whom she was referring. Then, she realized who this unexpected guest was, and she prepared her mind for meeting the man who would accompany her for the rest of her assignment.

William Evans.

Chapter 8

Waiting for her in the study was Will Evans, a man Chesca had not seen or heard of in years, and even during her time at Athena Academy she had never personally come into contact with him.

From Christine Evans's description, she could mildly recollect who he was, but it had been so many years her memory of him was based on fragments in time, odds and ends of moments that didn't reflect the man she saw before her.

Before making an entrance, she took a moment to get a glimpse of her new partner from her stance in the hall. She wanted to know what she was working with.

He looked different.

Then, Chesca supposed, so did she. It had been about

a decade since her time at Athena, and time had its way of changing a person's appearance. Though, in this case, time had served William well.

"You must be Will," she said, finally making a move to introduce herself.

His aquamarine eyes stared back at her as she took in his dark tan, traced his height of more than six feet, and assessed the reddish, sand-colored hair on his head.

She guessed the highlighted strips in his hair were a result of spending a good deal of time in the sun, though it was the intense color of his eyes that restricted her attention to directly in front of her.

"That I am." His smile broke through, and she could see he had warmed to her quickly, despite being an apparent hard-edged army man. "Francesca. I'd say nice to meet you, but my great-aunt tells me we likely crossed paths years ago."

"I don't really remember," Chesca said, as Will laughed heartily.

He calmed his humor to speak. "Nice to know I'm so memorable."

"You know what I—"

"I know what you meant," he said, letting his smile show his earnestness and good nature. "Honestly, that was so long ago. I'd think it a bit strange had you remembered me after all those years."

"Yes, I suppose so."

A slight curl in the corner of his mouth revealed a strange quality to this man's method of nonverbal communication and Chesca did her best to get a feel for his character from the get-go. She wanted to know what kind of person she would be spending some very important time with.

Though she trusted the intent and concern of Christine Evans, and of Delphi, Chesca had already made up her mind prior to Will's arrival that if she sensed a major personality conflict—such as an attempt by her so-called protector to outplay her plans for the case—she'd be honest about it and ask for someone else.

After all, she didn't want to waste time making clear how she expected to work on this case. She was used to working on her own and knew her downfall was not always doing the best with teamwork. Thankfully, she could see Will was an upstanding guy who was just doing what he was sent here to do.

In a strange way, she was pleased to see he had a sense of humor. Though she didn't fancy herself very funny, she did appreciate his attempts to make her feel comfortable in his presence. Plus, it was something Chesca had learned was integral on the job.

Between her own chosen profession and the cases she worked on regularly with the FBI, Chesca was faced with disaster, death and devastation with just about every case she handled. Her mentors at the Bureau, and her coworkers, often reminded her how corny some of the personalities could be at the strangest of times.

To outsiders, it might seem strange to be amidst a group of professionals dealing with death and murder and crime and hear them laugh about life, make puns about death, and joke even at the sidelines of a crime scene, but…it was human nature. It was a necessary coping mechanism. A person could laugh off some stress, deal with the harsh realities of the world, and save herself from going batty over what some members of society were capable of.

In a short amount of time, Chesca had learned the most warped senses of humor and unique personality traits could be found in any homicide squad room, and she was glad to have this hint of humanity spotted in her short-term partner Will Evans. Clearly, he had seen his share of the world and what darkness it could hold.

What she wasn't too sure about was how the war had actually affected him, if at all.

Of course it must have on some level, she knew, as there was no way a person could fight the fight without adjusting something within their psyche. It wasn't natural to see so much chaos on a regular basis and there was always the risk one would feel as though nothing could ever be done to stop it. But she wasn't sure if Will coming off the wounded list meant more to him personally, and she hoped for the best with him, and *for him.*

She knew one thing, though. She could trust him.

It was in his eyes.

And she knew anyone Christine sent would have the heart of a warrior and the soul of an angel.

As she looked at him, as she watched him make himself comfortable perusing the many stacks of books in the library, she was beginning to piece together memories she didn't realize she possessed.

She recalled seeing photographs of him, the few times she'd been called into Christine's office at the academy. Thinking back on it, Francesca could recall the neatly framed candid snapshots of Will and his youthful friends, sitting around campfires, or holding up hunting rifles.

While Chesca attended Athena, Will would have been just a few years her senior, spending his time in the swampland, being just like any other outdoorsy boy—out to strut testosterone in the wilderness.

She also knew his preoccupations didn't extend much further, though he may have outgrown the backyard landscape. He'd served in the army, but the man now standing in front of Chesca differed greatly from other army men she had met throughout her career. He didn't seem to be the clean-cut, uniform type.

He was slightly disheveled, though not at all in a messy or unclean sort of manner. He just seemed at ease, as if he didn't have to present himself as anything other than a good old boy from the South.

"What do you know, Will?" she asked candidly, wondering what, if anything, Christine had said about his purpose in joining her.

"Straight to the point. I like that," he said, then took a seat in one of the matching wingback chairs Chesca normally saw her father sit in after a late-night meal and a glass of brandy.

It was odd to see a young man such as Will sitting

in her father's place, but she focused her attentions to his response.

He slouched back into the comfort of the chair, as though he knew she was analyzing every move he made and making an estimation of his personality.

"I know something must be heating up, for an FBI profiler to get in on it." Then, stretching his arms along the top of the plush fabric, into a truly casual pose, he said, "I know from my great-aunt that Marion was being blackmailed. That her murder was arranged by someone who wanted to put an end to the Academy, among other things. And I suspect you're on the hunt for one such person. How's that?"

Could Will really know that much about what had happened to Marion, or was he just putting clues together he may have picked up from his aunt and on the rumor circuit? There was no way to tell for sure.

Though if he was going to follow her around while she set out to uncover the truth about blackmailers and assassins, he might as well get the crib notes on the matter.

There would naturally be some things to hold back, as part of her Oracle assignment, but it seemed to Chesca that Will already knew the basics. A little more wouldn't jeopardize her safety. And, at this point, she needed all the help she could get.

"First, I have to correct you," Chesca said, taking the seat opposite him to get more comfortable in the conversation. Will had so easily made himself at home in a place Chesca knew to be socially stuffy and less than inviting. She wanted to ensure he did feel comfortable in her presence, and she'd do the best she could to make him feel a part of her hunt. "I'm in this for personal reasons, not in an official FBI capacity."

"Understood."

"Yes, Marion was being blackmailed." The words came slowly from Chesca, as it was still hard to fathom what the Athena founder must have gone through.

The news of her murder devastated everyone who knew her.

Marion Gracelyn was a forward-thinking senator in the 1970s and gained an incredible reputation as a prosecuting attorney right up until the time of her death, when she was murdered by Senator Eldon Waterton. She'd worked hard and was such an incredible woman, one who meant so much to each and every graduate, and continued to epitomize the very reason for the academy's existence. "By Arachne."

Will sat up, telling Chesca he was in fact genuinely interested in the details of the case, and not just for the sake of following orders from his great-aunt Christine. "I'm not familiar with Arachne. Is that a person or an organization?"

She laughed, slightly amused, despite the severity of the situation.

"Arachne may as well be an entire army, she's so well connected. From what I can tell," Chesca said, brushing a hand over her jeans to smooth out some creases, "her activities extend far beyond what any of us first imagined."

"And your job is to put a face to this name."

In Will's comment, Chesca detected a solemn but respectable tone, in which she saw acceptance, perhaps even appreciation, for the task she was assigned and his personal vow to assist her in his own way.

"I am to profile Arachne and determine whether she is one and the same as the Queen of Hearts assassin. From what I've been told thus far," she said, though she was still awaiting further information to arrive from Delphi, "in the sixties, Salvatore Giambi hired a female mercenary he refers to as the Queen of Hearts. Or at least that's what he copped to when 'fessing up to the Bureau."

Will settled back into a relaxed position and Chesca noted his attempt to measure his weight in the situation, how much he was intended to know, and then settle into some comfort in seeing Chesca's smile. He must have taken her response as a signal that it was okay to prod further.

Chesca respected that he was taking his time in getting to know how she worked, and in seeing that he didn't just react without thought. She could tell he sensed out situations before taking the next step, and she liked that about him.

"Who's this Giambi character?"

She took in a deep breath. Beth and Allison had each mentioned a few interesting tidbits about Giambi, and in addition to what she knew of him through her role in the FBI, it was evident Giambi was less than a stellar guy.

He was a handful who didn't take well to not having things go his way.

"He owns a casino and is notorious in the high-roller gambling circuit. Long history with him. Apparently he hired this assassin, possibly former CIA, to take care of a rival of his, but soon after became a target of blackmail."

It was easy to see why.

Francesca had learned Giambi was a busy man. He had made an attempt to murder his suspected blackmailer while she was in jail, but failed. His money-laundering career was only kept quiet while his blackmailer kept him out of the limelight with the IRS and FBI, obviously for a hefty price tag. And from what Allison had said of the Puerto Isla bank account, the regular payments were no chump change.

She was eager to receive further information from Delphi. If this character was former CIA, and if she was Jackie Cavanaugh, Chesca would have a few interesting twists and turns to follow up on. It was worth checking out.

"Allison's going to keep digging for me," was all she said for now.

"And that's why you came here?" Will asked. "To see where it all began?"

"Exactly," she said, making a mental note to clue him in to how her meetings with Brighton and Schneider went. For now, she wanted to get him up to speed on the intel she'd been given prior to arriving in the city.

She watched Will's reaction as she shared, "Giambi's

Queen of Hearts? She's believed to be former CIA with the code name Weaver. And guess what?"

"What?"

"Weaver and Giambi are both Boston born and bred."

"Small world."

"You have no idea," Chesca said, thinking of the information she'd learned earlier.

But as she prepared to share her findings from the university meetings, they were interrupted by one of Abigail Thorne's employees.

"Miss Thorne, your mother requests your presence. Dinner is about to be served in the dining hall."

Chesca caught herself swallowing a laugh. The dining hall.

She knew there was the option of having them gather in the regular dining room attached to the kitchen, but Chesca guessed with the arrival of Will Evans, Abigail Thorne would have insisted they dine in the formal room, complete with polished silver and fine china. It was her mother's preference to make any little event an occasion.

"Thank you, Marlena," Chesca said. "We'll be just another minute."

Then, turning to see the amused but mildly baffled look on Will's face, Chesca smiled. "Yes, in case you haven't noticed, my family prefers to keep things formal around here. But you're lucky."

"How's that?" Will asked.

"I'm betting my mother didn't give you a lecture about your jeans," Chesca said, shaking her head as she compared their clothing. "Guests get off the hook a lot easier than family."

"You look fine to me. You look good."

For some reason the words made Chesca feel uncomfortable. A flush of color rose to her cheeks. She quickly covered them with a hand, hoping Will didn't catch what she could feel from her insides.

It was such a simple comment. One that didn't mean anything. Yet for some reason it caused a reaction within her, and Chesca didn't like that. But she didn't want him to know that either.

"Thanks," she said, aiming to recover from the awkward moment. "My bags and all my clothing are at the hotel, which we need to go check out. I was advised not to go back until you arrived, but, well that's the excuse for the jeans."

"Perfectly understandable."

"Not if you're my mother."

"Hey, we all have them, and they all have their quirks," Will said, which made Chesca curl her lips with pleasure.

Will did his best to be at ease with her, and didn't make a big deal out of nothing. He was easygoing, carefree, and yet she could clearly see that didn't also imply he was lax about his work ethic. He was just a simple kind of guy, and she knew that would make working with him much easier.

"You were saying," Will asked. "There was something else you picked up on today?"

"Yeah, you're not going to believe this," Chesca said.

She was thankful Will brought the conversation back around to something that would level her sudden awkward mannerisms. "I went to the university today and ended up talking to two different folks from Computer Sciences who had an awful lot to say about a student from some time ago."

"That fit the description of who you're looking for?"

"So far. And I got a name."

Chesca couldn't believe the expression that lit up on Will's face. He hardly knew her, had little personal attachment to this assignment other than following Christine's request, and yet he was genuinely pleased to hear such positive news come from Chesca's lips.

He smiled and nodded as he asked, "Anything you can work with?"

"Oh, yes. We're going to be checking out Jackie Cavanaugh. And, because I know your next question, you're going to love hearing this," Chesca said, pleased to see Will's interest in her teasing ways of sharing information. "The Cavanaugh family? Mob. All the way. How's that for a day's work?"

Will shook his head at the news. "No kidding."

"Not in the slightest," Chesca said as she finally got up from her comfortable seat to make their way to dinner. "So, I hope you're as good as they say you are. Who knows what kind of fun we'll be running into out here?"

Will stretched his lean legs as he joined Chesca through the door and followed her down the hall. "But that's the kind of fun I like. Plus, I may know how to take a bullet or two, but I don't intend on doing it again, nor letting you feel the pain. So you can count on me."

"I have a feeling I can," Chesca said, though as she said the words, she felt her cheeks color again and she was grateful Will was a few steps behind her so he wouldn't see.

Just then, Abigail Thorne rounded the hallway with a stern frown directed at Chesca, then a polite smile adopted quickly for the sake of their guest.

"We're ready for you, if you're able to join us," Chesca's mother said in a perturbed voice.

"Yes, thank you Mother," Chesca began to say, though Abigail Thorne didn't wait for an answer before turning her back to them and returning to the dining hall.

Chesca slowed her step and looked at Will. "By the way, my mother can be terribly impatient."

"Ah, that's nothing," he said, but Chesca smiled as she shook her head, thinking how little he could read the infamous Abigail Thorne.

She recognized Will came from the same background as Christine Evans, but she also knew that while the Evans family might have a respectable and highly regarded family tree, they were not of the crowd with which Abigail Thorne preferred to merge—those extra proud of their good fortune, in a high-and-mighty sort of way.

Chesca pegged him for the kind of guy who couldn't care less how much money a person had, or what they did with it, and she liked that about him immediately.

"Oh, you say that now. Wait until morning when

Roger is reaching up into your inseam, and my mother is telling you what pants to wear."

Chesca laughed at the confused look on Will's face as he innocently asked, "I'm sorry. What?"

Chapter 9

During the family dinner, Will had entertained his hosts. Despite Abigail Thorne's curiosity about why it was he had joined her daughter so out of the blue, Will was able to keep the conversation off his work.

Chesca appreciated that. As Will no doubt understood, any mention of his role as a bodyguard would send off red flags to her mother about the potentially dangerous case she was working, and that would have only caused more grief for her parents, who were already annoyed that their only daughter chose to work in law enforcement.

Neither Abigail nor Dorian Thorne were oblivious to the occupational hazards involved in Chesca's chosen field, but the topic was rarely discussed. They didn't want to think about her life being put in jeopardy at times, let alone of the other side effects such as stress, little sleep and a definite lack of social time, which was likely what bothered her mother the most.

Will had clearly picked up on the residual parental resentment and tensions felt across the table when the topic of professions came up. But to Chesca's delight, he stood up for her field, which was his as well, and did his best to keep an even and peaceful playing field during the meal.

What was nice was that she was also able to learn a bit more about him without subjecting him to interrogation. She was curious to know who he was, how his mind worked, why he chose to do what he did, and the most beneficial part of sharing the family dinner with him was allowing her family to ask all the questions, letting her sit back and simply absorb the information.

Will shared a bit of his own family past, telling them about how he grew up around Fort Benning, Georgia, and spent most of his youth outdoors. Chesca's father nodded along as Will described the endless summer days spent fishing, hunting and exploring the swamps south of Columbus, and despite having not done that himself, Dorian Thorne took a pleasing interest in hearing about such a laid-back life. It was a contrast to his lifetime of business suits and monetary pursuits.

It was interesting to hear how Will made his way around Georgia, Florida and South Carolina, and Chesca could almost feel the joy in his voice as he spoke of his personal interests and viewpoints on living in small towns. She herself had never experienced the friendships he described, the family relationships where everyone not only got along, but genuinely liked each other's company. It was refreshing to hear someone other than a Thorne take up conversation at the table.

Though as a bodyguard for the U.S. Army, Will rarely gave hints as to what he did or for whom. Chesca knew part of that was out of respect for his work, and part of that was just his personality in not being someone who rambled on endlessly about being some great hero with war stories but little personality. Instead, Will seemed quite charming, and handled the questions from Abigail and Dorian with grace, dignity and humor.

For their part, Chesca's parents did well to extend polite nods and mediocre smiles, and were curious to the point of seeming interested, but thankfully they had not overstepped boundaries. In a way, Chesca supposed that may have also had to do with their lack of interest in getting to know too much about how Chesca's world operated. Keeping it simple and superficial with Will saved them from fully understanding their daughter's occupation.

Will was gracious, however, when it came to describing his family. Though Chesca could relate very little to his upbringing, she was pleased to hear the true respect he had for his kin, and how happy he was to talk about them. He was truly a family man.

It was interesting to hear about his great-aunt Christine Evans from his perspective as well. Though he told stories for the benefit of Abigail and Dorian Thorne, it was nice for Chesca to hear about another side of the woman she had come to know through the Athena Academy.

"She may be in her sixties," Will said with light in his eyes, "but she is as fiery as a teenager and as energetic as one too."

After dinner, the four of them sat around the fireplace, soaking in the evening and capping it off with a cocktail. It was tradition in the Thorne residence, and Will made himself perfectly at home by reversing the interrogation and asking all kinds of questions of Chesca's parents. Though her mother was quick to shut him down, other than to brag about the Thorne Family Foundation and the upcoming spring gala, Dorian did his part in going on about business affairs and giving insight about various stocks he suggested Will check out.

It was interesting to see Will dive right into conversation with what Chesca viewed as something far from his own preferred social circle, but Will held his own, blended well, and never once came off as phony, or seemed as though he was just being polite. He was good with people. He must have developed that trait early on, as a strong member of the Evans family, and carrying on his role in following the footsteps of the other career lifers in his army family.

When the Thorne elders excused themselves to call

it a night, Will and Chesca got right back to work on laying out the basics of what Chesca had learned thus far and what their plan of attack would be for the following day.

"Once we get the wardrobe malfunctions taken care of," Will said in humor, "what first? Any preferences?"

With her files by her side, as they sat outside on the covered patio, enjoying the spring evening with a hot cup of coffee to keep their blood warm, Chesca thought. "I have an appointment set up with Major Crimes to see what we can dig up about Jackie Cavanaugh. I want to see what they know about her past, if there was any confirmation of her involvement with the CIA, or a clue to how she got involved with Salvatore Giambi, assuming she is our girl."

Will nodded his head, and stretched out his legs as he slouched into the wooden lounger. The weather was damp, cool, and provided evidence of a rain shower on the way, but with Boston being the recipient of any number of wind systems, the locals knew the only thing to expect with the weather was never knowing what to expect. "And it's a given, I think, that the vandalism to the rental car was deliberate. Maybe they'll have something to say about that, too."

"For sure. Though what scares me is how soon that happened after I arrived in town. I mean, I only just got here. I can see something like that happening after a day or two, once someone gets wind of me sniffing after a trail. But so soon?"

It was something that concerned her. Chesca had only been in the city overnight, after a brief stay at the hotel room before heading out to see Brighton. And yet someone had already been on her tail, knowing she was looking into something they obviously didn't want her to know. It was enough to fuel her ambitions even more.

"At least we know to keep our guard up." Will held his coffee mug close to his chest, the steam from the hot beverage wafting in front of his face, as the mist in the cool air contrasted with the liquid. "And we know not to take our chances. I have a feeling this is one woman we don't want to mess with."

"If she has this mob family too, it won't be just her we're dealing with," Chesca noted, having considered this before. "Technically, we're on their turf now, so if she's close to them, it'll be natural instinct for them to keep her safe from us."

He nodded. And Chesca noticed the solemn and contemplative manner in which Will seemed to think. He didn't say much, but his mannerisms said more than his words. Chesca could see Will was typically a quiet guy, one who chose his words wisely, but that didn't hold him back from carrying on decent conversation.

"And we'll need to clear your hotel room out, gather your things, make sure nothing's gone missing. You have all the important stuff on you though, I'd assume."

"You'd assume correctly. Laptop, notes, never left my side. Thankfully."

As they discussed potential places to seek out further

information on the CIA recruit, who also might have been known as Jackie Cavanaugh, Chesca thought of how lucky she was that Christine had sent her great-nephew. With Will, she'd lucked out. From all external appearances, he held no potential for getting in her way, didn't appear to be a threat to her personal space needs, and didn't have the ego she would have guessed for a high-profile bodyguard.

He was, in fact, a treat. Compared to what she had conjured up in her mind, he was as easygoing as they came and she was grateful she would have his company for this case.

"I know this is your thing," Will said, and Chesca wondered if maybe she had been wrong and judged him too soon. Did he have a personal agenda he was only now going to share?

"Yes, go on," she said with some hesitation.

"But it's important to me too, you know. My great-aunt, she's wonderful. And I know how much Athena Academy means to her, meant to Marion Gracelyn. And it's pretty crappy to see all that's happened, ya know?"

Chesca smiled. Nodded her head in agreement. She reminded herself she needed to trust her gut. Had she done that, she wouldn't be second-guessing Will's perspectives, as she had just done. Instead, he was again proving what an upstanding and earnest guy he was with a family-oriented heart.

"I know. And thank you. The Academy means a lot to me too, which is why I say this is more of a personal case than just something that falls under my professional scope."

"You must have enjoyed the Academy. I remember visiting and thinking what a cool place it was, and in seeing how much Christine loved that place, it really felt special," Will said, emitting some of the very emotions Chesca and her classmates had always felt.

"I was lucky. I can't imagine how my life would be had I not been invited to the Academy. That's where I really learned about life. Where I grew up," Chesca said, allowing Will to see some of her personal views and reflections on her upbringing. "Don't get me wrong, I know at face value, looking at this place, you'd think it'd be a great place to grow up. But, being a Thorne isn't all it's cracked up to be."

"I got the gist of that," Will said, chuckling but still maintaining his respect for his hosts. "I could tell there was some pretty historic tension between you and your folks, though it's always like that. Parents always hope for one thing and then they can either accept what they're given or fight against it all their lives. I was lucky, and though I can see you had it good on that superficial level, I can also see how Athena Academy might've been your refuge. And I can see how they would have picked up on how special you are."

Instead of blushing this time, Chesca took the direct route and looked Will in the eyes. Perhaps it was the liquid courage she had consumed, or the lateness of the hour and the dimness in the lighting, but this time she wanted to see his face as she absorbed such a compliment.

"You hardly know me. How do you know I'm special?" she asked, curious to see how he'd answer.

"The Academy recruited you. I may not know you well yet, but I do know Athena Academy and what they stand for. If they sought you out, it was for a reason. And I'm betting they think they made the right decision and consider themselves lucky for having spotted you."

Though her humor wanted to make a quick-witted retort to his commentary, Chesca knew what an honor it was to be an Athena grad and she didn't want to make a mockery of what her alma mater stood for. Instead, she absorbed the compliment with grace, and thanked Will for it. "That was nice of you to say, and you're right. I'd do anything to pay them back for the education I was given."

"You will. We both will. We'll find what you need to settle your assignment."

A quiet pride filled Chesca's heart. Will was right. This assignment was a great way for Chesca to show her appreciation for all she had gained from Athena Academy. The best memories she possessed of her youth, and of her life, were those surrounding the time she had spent growing and learning, thriving in such an encouraging environment. And she knew without a doubt that other young women needed—deserved—to have the same opportunity. She would make sure of that.

As her cell phone rang, Chesca had a surge of adrenaline. Hoping it was Delphi calling to share information about the case, or connect their prey to the CIA, she didn't hesitate to answer the unknown caller ID.

"Thorne."

Will watched with interest as Chesca listened, and in turn she kept her eyes on him as she carried on the conversation. Though to him it likely seemed like a cryptic call with Chesca's few words of "Right. Okay. I'll see what I can do," being just about as much as she got in, and never once did she let her tone show evidence of success.

When she clicked off her phone, she let out a sigh and let her thoughts formulate. She knew Will was eager to hear the news she'd received, but it was not what she'd expected.

"Everything okay?" he asked.

"Fine." Though her tone came out shakier than she would have liked. When Will pressed her with a waiting look, she knew she had to confess. "That was the field office in Baton Rouge. I just came back from profiling a serial killer and we thought we got him."

"Thought? As in they don't actually have him?"

Her head hurt just thinking about it.

"Oh, they got someone all right. Hell, I stabbed him right there, leaving a fresh blood trail for them to follow. I was there when he was taken into custody, for goodness sake."

She had to pause for a moment, realizing her agitation against the field agents would do no good now. "Loopholes. That's what I'm told. Seems none of the evidence actually ties this guy to the murder scenes. The victim we found is in no condition to identify the man who assaulted her, not yet anyway. Of course they're going to charge him with something, having snuck up on me and uttered ungentlemanly threats. But as for the murders? They don't have a single thread on him. Yet. Though they will, if I can help it."

It was beyond comprehension. Agent Sharland had informed her that while the man clearly had Chesca believing he was in fact their guy, the matter at hand was purely circumstantial.

While she had gathered his DNA through stabbing him with her knife, there was no DNA left at any of the previous crime scenes to match it to. And since he didn't kill the sixth victim, nor was he found standing directly next to her, there wasn't enough to make it stick.

Circumstantial. She hated that word.

She knew better. They knew better. It wasn't coincidence the man happened to be at the scene of what was expected to be the seventh murder. At least these lesser charges would keep him within arm's reach as they rallied for more tangible evidence to nail him. She would see to that.

"You need to go back to Baton Rouge?"

Chesca looked at Will, knowing her assignment from Delphi would only be that much more pressing with an open serial case to her credit as well. But, she'd been known to multitask before. It simply meant she would have to retain her mental focus, her brainpower. The very reason for which Oracle had recruited her would now be put to the test.

"Possibly. In time. For now, we're keeping focused on what we're here to do," Chesca said, thinking of how things could work out. "I'll review some of my notes on that case while we're in between tasks on this one."

"Sounds good," Will said, keeping his voice calm considering the not-so-good news. "Hey, I'm sorry to hear that it didn't work out the way you wanted. It has to be frustrating."

Chesca shrugged her shoulders. "It can be. But this one shouldn't be. There has to be something I already know that can help this one get shut down. I mean, come on. We got the guy, for goodness sake. I know it. They know it. Hell, he knows it. I just need something. One thing that will seal it."

Though it might have seemed like a minuscule gesture to some, when Will handed Chesca the plate of chocolate chip cookies they'd brought outside to accompany their coffee, it meant a great deal to her. A small gesture, for sure, but there was little a good chocolate chip cookie couldn't placate.

She was frustrated. She was downright furious. But, that feeling would subside and be replaced by determination. If there was one thing Chesca understood about her line of work, it was that the legal system did not always equal the justice system. Just because the feds or cops nabbed someone, did not mean the courts would agree or be favorable toward their evidence.

But as always, Chesca would take the opportunity to find even more evidence, even more proof of what she already knew. The man who'd held a knife to her throat in Baton Rouge was their killer.

And if she had to get that close to him again to prove it, she would.

Chapter 10

As Will and Chesca were wrapping up their morning fashion consultation with Roger, one of Abigail's many employees informed Chesca a package had arrived to her attention. It was the information she had requested of Delphi, and Chesca couldn't wait to get her hands on it.

"Just a few more moments of patience," Roger requested of her, as she began to show signs of restlessness. "You know your dear mother would have my head if I didn't see to it that you were suitably attired for the gala."

"Roger, anything would have served the purpose," she replied, annoyed by the amount of effort everyone else seemed to think she needed in dressing for the annual occasion. "You know I don't care for all the fuss."

"I know, dear, but your mother—"

"Just…can we speed it up a bit, please?" she requested, keeping her posture straight and her body tight as Roger wrapped measuring tapes around the tulle-covered black evening gown he was trying to make fit her like a glove.

While she could admit the style was acceptable for an evening, she didn't see the need to make it magazine-perfect. She was definitely an off-the-rack kind of girl, content with whatever she could find in a local mall.

"I think it's looking pretty good," Will offered, as he sat in the lounge chair, already finished with his portion of the fitting.

Roger had quickly and easily suited up Will in a classic James Bond style tuxedo that, quite honestly, in Chesca's opinion, transformed the good old country boy into something modern and magnificent. He certainly cleaned up well.

"You know," Roger said, keeping his eyes on Chesca, but turning his attention to her partner, "I've dressed this family for more than a decade and this one always gives me the same tired old treatment of being Miss Fussy Pants."

"Fussy pants?" Will said, hardly holding back his laughter. "Chesca, I didn't realize you were a fussy pants."

"I'm not."

"Oh, she is," Roger said, priding himself on being able to divulge such insider information. "Unfortunately, it never works in my favor. Honestly, I bring her the best. Gucci. Dior. Chanel. And she treats them as equals. Seriously, this girl has no sense of what's what when it comes to fashion, other than knowing full well how hot she looks in black."

"I'd have to agree there." Will's eyes roamed the figure of his partner, and Chesca felt naked in front of him, despite the overabundance of fabric that adorned her body.

She checked out her own reflection in the mirror and while she did appreciate how the dress fit her in all the right places, she felt nervous under scrutiny, never being one to place much importance on fashion or personal appearances.

Beyond the obvious hygiene and classic styling she preferred, she tried her best to stray from the obsessive wardrobe planning her mother subjected her to any chance she got. She didn't want to inherit the sense that external appearances carried more weight than a person's heart and soul, and somehow that translated into avoiding over-the-top fashions and settling for basics she could rely on.

Roger's eyes were beaming with pleasure as he took in the compliment Will bestowed upon Chesca and accepted the credit to her looks as his. "She does have a fabulous body, and if she'd just show it off from time to time, maybe she'd remind herself of that."

"Roger, I don't need to show off anything," Chesca said, growing irritated with the focus on her and her appearance. "I like to keep it simple. Classic. Whatever's easy."

"I know, my dear child, I know. Honestly, William,

you'd think she'd realize how lucky she has it. Any woman in the world would kill to have a personal shopper at her disposal providing the most fabulous of top designers, and yet Francesca Fussy Pants here is fighting me tooth and nail, year after year after year. It's enough to give me a headache."

Chesca laughed at Roger's drama. "You're giving me a headache. Are we done yet?"

Her clothier stepped back, glanced at her up and down, and nodded his head. "Yes, you may change back into those dreadful rags, Cinderella. I brought some jeans and—dare I say it—basics for you to make use of, at your mother's request. Go. Go on, get out of here before I change my mind and take this up another inch."

"That won't be necessary," Chesca said, stepping off the platform Abigail Thorne had permanently installed in the north side of her walk-in wardrobe years ago for the exact purpose of making things easier for Roger. "In case I didn't mention it, thank you. I appreciate your assistance."

His face was shocked as she leaned in to kiss him on the cheek. Roger breathed a sigh and then looked at Will. "She'll break your heart if you're not careful. Don't say I didn't warn you."

Chesca thought Will was being a good spirit when he replied, "Then I guess I'll take my chances," though for a moment she cringed at the thought of Roger going any further with sharing stories from her past. Thankfully, they had work to do and it wouldn't be an issue.

There had been male suitors in her past and she didn't

care to revive their place in her mind, or the emptiness they left in her heart.

Unfortunately, being a Thorne meant often being escorted to galas and fund-raisers by men Abigail or Dorian had picked. She wasn't enough of a socialite in the "right" circles, according to her parents, and often at the last minute she'd learn her date's identity, and how much she was supposed to like him.

Usually, it felt like any other duty she was obligated to perform for her parents.

But Chesca had had a relationship or two that almost felt right. There was a time when she'd found someone she liked, because she liked him, had met him on her own in natural circumstances, rather than under the forced conditions of the Thorne household.

Whether due to youth or timing or perhaps the planets not aligning in her favor, it didn't work out. And it was the one time Chesca let down her guard, got past some of her intimacy issues and just went with the flow. She got burned, and as a result, she now thought twice before going down that road again.

As a forensic psychologist, she knew her own mind. She also knew she couldn't diagnose all of her own issues, but this one thing she knew. Since being disappointed with those she'd trusted at such a young age, of course it had scarred her and made her extra cautious with those she surrounded herself with, especially anyone she would consider getting close to.

Though she didn't feel it held her back in any way

that was cause for serious concern, she knew full well it was one of the reasons she chose to operate under her own terms, close herself off to much of a social life, and focus on work.

Work she could trust. Science didn't lie. Cases were methodical and there were laws she could work within. Social mores and expectations, dating, relationships, friendships outside of bonds she'd made at the Academy? There were so many uncertainties. So many unknown variables she couldn't predict. And she liked to play it safe. She was not fond of surprises. Especially ones that hurt.

"He was a treat," William said as the two of them headed out for the road to meet with the Major Crimes folks at police headquarters. During the drive, Chesca intended to catch up on whatever Delphi had sent via courier.

"That's an understatement for you, I bet," Chesca said. Though she was accustomed to Roger's directness and candor, she figured it was a bit more startling to an outsider.

"He was interesting. To say the least. But he had one thing right," Will said. "That dress was really nice on you. You'll look great at this ball thing we're going to. Which I can't believe I'm going to, but duty calls and all."

"Uh-huh, duty calls." Chesca knew it was a curve-ball for Will to hear he was attending the spring gala with her, but she'd also figured out that he wasn't all that upset about it. Since accepting the invitation from Abigail Thorne, Will had mentioned it enough times for

Chesca to realize he was actually looking forward to dressing up for the night.

And she was looking forward to seeing him dressed up as well. That tux had made him look…well, very nice.

"So, what's the news?"

Chesca had suggested Will drive so she could read through the files as they made their way to headquarters. As she flipped through some papers she could hardly believe some of the information she was privy to. It was amazing that Delphi was able to gather such information on short notice.

"Well, we know the connection between Salvatore Giambi and the Queen of Hearts. We also know the Queen of Hearts is likely this same person with the code name Weaver that the CIA recruited years ago."

"You can never have enough aliases," Will said, again showing his humor.

"The files say this Weaver person joined the military in the sixties, traveled around the world, got right in on the action," Chesca said, reading highlights from the package. "Weaver knew about the Combat Zone, and with her being so great with computers and having little heart but a black one, she got into blackmailing. And, I know serial blackmailing is such a tricky thing to profile, but from what it sounds like, we're on the trail of the right woman, I'd say."

What Chesca wasn't able to share with Will was how impressed she was with Oracle and the work of Delphi.

Though she knew how Oracle conducted their

business and how assignments came based on what the organization needed at the time, she was never more impressed than she was at this point, as she read the highly sensitive information given to her.

In the package sent by Delphi, by an Athena Academy courier, was the entire CIA dossier on Jackie Cavanaugh. It wasn't so much the information that perplexed Chesca, it was the meaning it implied. For Delphi to get her hands on CIA files? Oracle must be more sophisticated and connected than she'd imagined.

As an FBI agent, Chesca knew she wouldn't have such an easy time rounding up that kind of information. And yet, Delphi was able to do so without a hitch? Chesca was not only impressed, she was overwhelmed with awe at how powerful a network Oracle must be. That was serious government agency information in her hands, no doubt collected secretly, or under some pretty specific conditions. The CIA didn't go around handing out information to just anyone. Could Delphi really have that high a computer security clearance with all government agencies?

If that was the case, Chesca knew whoever Delphi was in reality must have some pretty significant friends to call on when needed.

"You mind?" Will asked, as he flipped on the radio dial and surfed for something to listen to during the drive. They were less than an hour away from headquarters and the day was mild, though again overcast, and Chesca didn't have a problem with feeding their minds some casual background music to make the journey pass more quickly.

"That's fine. Just nothing with too heavy of a beat. I want to be able to hear my thoughts," she said.

Will gave off a subtle laugh. "Do I look like someone who needs a fast beat and a lot of bass?"

As he settled into a station that broadcast a mix of country, blues and contemporary rock, Chesca nodded her head. "That's pretty much how I would have pegged you," she said. "Something classic and mellow."

Kind of like his personality, she thought.

Though she was only getting to know Will and didn't know much of his personal life, she could tell he was the kind of guy who didn't get worked up over much of anything. She would have guessed that even in stressful situations, high-profile action and military crises, he would just roll with the punches and do what he needed to do without causing a fuss. To Chesca, Will seemed casual in just about every outlook he shared on life, work and play.

"Take it easy and have a good time," is what he had said over dinner the night before, causing Abigail Thorne to raise her brows in judgment. Though it sounded like a good philosophy to Chesca.

"What about you?" Will asked, taking a corner smoothly as they headed into a historic part of the neighborhood. At least the drive would be visually pleasing, with so many local attractions and beautiful architecture to admire.

"What about me?"

"Music, I mean. What do you like?"

Chesca thought about it and cringed. She wasn't sure how outdated she was on what was hot, what was on the charts, and what was the common fad of the day with most people. She rarely turned on the radio and never downloaded music. She had given up on trying to be cool years ago. Anything she liked was by default, just hearing something and judging it on its own merit, deciding whether she liked it for what it was, instead of what genre it fell into.

"I don't know. I guess I like classic rock. I do like some jazz, I'll admit, and some classical. Actually, I really like classical, but I don't know anything about it. All I know is it's easy to work to as far as background music goes, catching up on paperwork at late hours of the night when you just want something other than the sound of your computer keys to listen to. It doesn't get in the way, know what I mean?"

"Sure, I get it. No vocals, smooth sounds, but lots of emotions. Probably makes you work faster."

"You have some interesting theories, my friend," Chesca said, amused at how easy it was to talk with Will. It was hard to tell what kind of working relationship she would have with someone until she shared space with them in a car. Dead silence could turn uncomfortable, too much chatter could be unbearable, and it wasn't often she found someone who understood the fine art of balance.

But Will understood it perfectly. He was easy to talk

to, but Chesca didn't feel the need to make small talk to fill the void. It felt comfortable sharing space with him. As though they had known each other for years. It felt normal to spend time in one another's company.

In any other circumstance, Chesca felt as though she could have become friends with Will. He was the kind of person she could see herself hanging out with.

Of course, she knew their time together would be limited, and focused on work, but had they met at a social event back home in Virginia, she would have been happy to call him friend.

One thing for sure, he made the drive very pleasant. The hour passed quickly and by the time they got through discussing how it was they each came to preferring their particular types of music, they had arrived outside the Boston police headquarters and found a place to park. That in itself was a triumph for the day, with parking at a premium in the city and far too many cars hankering for a limited number of spots.

The clerk at the reception desk was less than welcoming when the two of them approached to announce their arrival, but that was something Chesca was used to. With the amount of strange complaints and bizarre characters the main desk came across day in and day out, it was understandable to miss out on a friendly smile from a desk clerk.

"Waters," Chesca said, requesting the sergeant she had set up an appointment to see.

After making it through security clearance and

being escorted to the appropriate floor by a uniformed officer, Will and Chesca took a seat in the hall outside Major Crimes. As they waited for Sergeant Waters to wrap up a phone call, Will took the time to clarify Chesca's intentions.

"So Baton Rouge. How's that going to work out for you?"

The sigh was deep and hard. Chesca had felt the frustration regarding that case all through her sleeping hours, tossing and turning as she tried to come up with something. She knew she had a piece of the puzzle in her mind, but it might take some time to think of an alternate angle with the competing case of Arachne on her brain.

"I may have to review some evidence with Forsythe," she said, referring to her friend and fellow Athena Force alumnus, Alex Forsythe. "She's incredible, and there was enough physical evidence from that scene that perhaps the clue is already there, what we need, and we just need to look harder."

"You're confident then?"

Chesca met Will's glance with an expression she hoped he would believe. "Don't I have to be? I refuse to accept that we just don't have it. I'm betting it's one of those things that's so dang obvious, you kick yourself after the fact, wondering how the heck you missed it in the first place."

"Like when something's staring you right in the eyes and you can't see it for your own faults of perception," Will said, taking Chesca aback, wondering what he had implied. The way the words rolled off his tongue, and the tone he used, something rang differently in her ears than Will's usual pitch and she was trying to get a feel for what the difference was when they were interrupted, in a welcome way, by Waters.

"Thorne?" the Sergeant asked and Chesca got up to shake hands and introduce William Evans. Then they followed the sergeant into a room that could have represented any squad room in the country.

It was the same as any old briefing room, crowded with chairs and mismatched desks, files piled in some makeshift organized manner, but the stacks upon stacks of them verified that this was one busy office.

Chesca hated how sometimes television and movies glamorized the working situations of police stations and federal offices. Fact was, very few agencies and stations had the kind of funds to furnish their offices with anything other than worn-out, used and refurbished pieces. Budgets were behind any decorating scheme, and it was obvious these folks in this unit were catered to with the same method of trimming the expenses.

However, Chesca also knew a department's merit couldn't be judged on its esthetics. It was the brain power that mattered. Any unit was only as good as the people working in it. For their interests, she hoped Waters was top-notch and would be able to help them out with some priceless information.

"Cavanaughs, huh?" Waters said, digging through a

stack of cream-colored file folders and pulling one out to set on the top of the desk. "Hope you like to read."

The files were massive, though it wasn't a surprise to Chesca, nor obviously to Will. Knowing the mob connection, as they did now, Chesca figured there would be a long history to review. Or at least she'd hoped.

"I've pulled the case files on the murder of an old Mafia don," Waters said as Chesca began to flip through pages dating back years upon years. "You're welcome to see what you need to see, but before you copy anything, give me a heads-up. Protocol, you understand."

"Not a problem," she said, happy that he seemed open to disclosing whatever information she desired. She could have had a rough time, getting someone who didn't personally care for federal agents, but Waters seemed like a decent enough guy, ready to be of assistance.

"I'm mostly interested in Jackie, and I've heard she's got a long history of working people," Chesca said.

"Yeah, she's something. Keep in mind, though, her brothers are a nasty bunch. They're running down every street they can get control over, operating a bunch of petty setups out to make a buck and heading up a gang or two in particularly careless ways," Waters said, flipping over some pages to show mug shots of Jackie's brothers.

Seeing those and being able to put faces to names would certainly be useful if Will and Chesca were going to hit the streets looking for more info on Jackie. Last thing they would want is to unknowingly come into contact with one of her family members and set themselves up for a bad situation.

"Of course, you can guess," he said, leaning into the table with a casual slouch, hunching his small frame over into what was likely the same position he sat in regularly, typing up reports and reviewing files. "Mostly drugs and prostitution for them. And more drugs. How Jackie fit into that, I can't tell you. But the boys, it's all they know. Good thing is, they only deal it out to gangs, they don't use themselves."

At least she wouldn't be fighting off some cracked-up mob heir whose only personal belongings were a gun and a bag of coke. Drugs you can't reason with. Mob members? At least Chesca felt she had a fighting chance with those.

"Any news on the car?" Will asked, and Chesca lifted her glance from the files to watch Waters's response.

"Likely them. Can't prove it. Probably sent out a kid from one of their gangs to take care of it." The sergeant met Chesca's eyes with seriousness. "You do much broadcasting that you'd be in town for her?"

Chesca gave him a rundown of her arrival into Boston, a timeline of what she'd done and where, and neither of them could figure how the Cavanaugh boys, or anyone else for that matter, would have had enough time to put the pieces together and take action.

"My advice then," Waters said, "is to keep it low, keep it quiet, and get what you need before getting out of town. You piss one of them off, you'll know it. But there won't be a lot I can do for you if you're dead."

Chesca nodded and looked at Will. "Got it. But we would like to get some information about their general whereabouts. If we can check some of the neighborhoods, maybe find someone that remembers Jackie but has a beef with her over something. Who knows? Maybe someone out there has something to say and has been waiting for an opportunity to say it."

Sergeant Waters outlined a few key areas in the city where Will and Chesca could try to seek out Jackie Cavanaugh's history, and while he printed off some documents for them to take with them, Will gave Chesca a nudge.

"Well, what do you think?"

"I don't know whether to be pleased or not," Chesca said, weighing the information she now had in her possession. "On one hand, we've got a good grasp on who we're after. Someone who was raised in a mob and is accustomed to street crime, somewhat organized crime, and the world of drugs, guns and prostitution. Also, someone who has no problem blackmailing lovers, employers and friends. And, someone who can clearly maneuver from country to country, leaves behind a collection of identities, and yet manages to leave little evidence as to her existence and who she is."

Will stood up from his chair as they were called over by Waters to gather the documents so they could head out on their hunt. "So, what's the downside of all that?"

"Someone like that, Will," Chesca said, knowing the weight of her words, "implies we're not just after a murderer. We're after a sociopath. And sociopaths play by their own rules."

Chapter 11

By definition, Chesca knew sociopaths had no reasoning when it came to widely accepted social norms.

There was a lack of perception about what other reasonable members of society did or how the world worked, in the sense that their behavior had no subconscious moral code to back often dangerous decisions. Whatever a sociopath opted to do was out of their own accord, regardless of whether or not the rest of society viewed it as acceptable. And Chesca knew she couldn't just reason with that kind of person, as the argument just wouldn't compute.

That, of course, was by definition. By her own personal experience, she knew it was fact. Many times she had encountered an individual who was so removed from society, so locked in their own mind, that they were not only a danger to those around them, they were also a danger to themselves.

Lack of a moral conscience. Lack of a social code. Antisocial behavior. No moral responsibility.

No matter how it was defined, it wasn't simple.

That was the issue.

Chesca could never know what to expect from this sort of criminal. There was nothing she could predict, which meant she had to treat everything as a possibility in order to cover all the bases.

Regardless of Jackie Cavanaugh's textbook description, Chesca vowed to find out as much as she could to provide as much information as possible for Delphi. Once she could provide more clues as to who this woman was and how she operated, it would be a lot easier to find her, and put an end to all she had been trying to accomplish in bringing down the much-loved Athena Academy. And, most important, Chesca would find some justice for the deaths of Marion Gracelyn and all the others affected by Arachne's wicked ways.

It was just after noon by the time Chesca and Will pulled up to the hotel where Chesca had left her belongings. While she hadn't physically been there since her phone call with Delphi, she had kept contact with the hotel manager, updating her credit card information and requesting the room not be made up or cleaned in any way. She wanted to be able to see the room exactly as she had left it, or however it might appear to her now after abandoning it to criminal possibilities.

"This is it?" Will asked as they approached the corner unit on the second floor.

Chesca nodded her head and handed him the key.

From the hallway, there were no signs of forced entry and to all outside viewers nothing would seem out of the ordinary here. Chesca began to wonder if they would learn nothing was behind their concern.

But as Will made a quiet entrance and secured the first few steps, he invited Chesca to join him in the hotel room and she saw Delphi's precautionary suggestion had likely worked out to her best interest.

Though the room was far from ransacked, it was clear someone had made an unlawful entry into her suite.

She distinctly recalled keeping all windows and doors locked, yet the large window leading off the balcony now had a torn screen, with a straight slit cut down the side that would have provided access to the lock.

A few of the dresser drawers were slightly ajar, and despite Chesca not being a neat freak about things, she knew she wouldn't have left those open, not even an inch.

The mattress had been shifted a bit, letting her know whoever was in here was accustomed to finding important information—and likely cash—tucked away out of plain sight. That wouldn't have been the case with her, since she left nothing for anyone to find. She was feeling as though her personal space had been invaded with a touch of creepiness. Who knows how things would have happened had she returned to the hotel room just one more time. Would she have come face to face with a criminal? A thief? A murderer?

She was glad she hadn't found out the hard way.

"It's all clear," Will said, coming back to the main room from the bathroom. "Not too bad of a mess, but I think it's obvious someone isn't looking to make friends with you anytime quick."

Chesca kept her focus on the mess and sifted through her personal belongings. "Doesn't appear that anything's missing. Kind of makes you wonder…"

"That never did anyone any good," Will said.

"What's that?"

He gave her a knowing look. "Wondering what could have happened, what could have been. Hindsight doesn't mean all that much to me."

Whether it was the statement itself or the way he said it, Chesca took a moment's glance away from her work to take in Will and think about what sort of person he was, or who she perceived him to be. There was something intriguing about him that made Chesca curious as to how he'd become the man she saw before her, and what sort of life he led when no one was looking. She wondered if he was so laid-back, unaffected and modestly proactive in his life as he evidently was in his ways of conducting work.

She wanted to know how he'd fallen into becoming a highly regarded bodyguard for the U.S. Army, protecting higher-ups on very sensitive journeys. Was it something he pursued, she wondered, or was he recruited when somēone spotted some specific traits or skills he possessed?

And despite his muscular physique, Chesca wondered what special physical capabilities he had, since he was not of a bulky frame, nor did he look as though he were the sort of person who worked out in a gym every day, increasing his weight and girth.

Instead, Will had a solid frame that matched his height—likely a few inches over six feet, Chesca estimated—and had a rangy, slightly rough outback look to his presence. Though as he described his youthful upbringing in the south, Chesca imagined a lifetime of hunting and fishing would get him in decent shape, and no matter how he got into the army, he would have been sure to keep up a regular routine of some variation.

As Chesca gathered her items of clothing and stuffed them into her one suitcase, an unexpected thought hit her.

She was attracted to Will.

It took her aback for a moment to accept that realization, not knowing if it was an attraction to him as a colleague, or if it was something else entirely different. Whatever it was, the moment made her redirect her thoughts and focus on the task at hand. She didn't want to entertain the possibilities roaming around in her mind as he assisted her in cleaning up her belongings. It simply wasn't something to consider. She was here to work.

"What are you smiling about?" she asked him, when

she caught his eyes looking at her through the reflection of the mirror. It was an interesting image to take in.

She could see her own presence in the reflected background, with Will up close to the mirror, facing it, but catching a glance at the entire room behind him.

Whatever he was thinking, he wasn't giving Chesca the satisfaction of replying with anything more than a simple, but coy, "Nothing. You think you got everything?"

She scanned the room once more and when they were satisfied everything was in order, Chesca and Will loaded the car before taking a walk into the hotel's restaurant, where they could discuss some of what had happened, and review in more detail the CIA dossier sent by Delphi.

Once seated, and once coffee had been served, they made small talk prior to ordering some lunch. Breakfast had been served at the Thorne house bright and early, and the day would be long, so they had agreed to refuel their bodies before heading out to search the streets.

One thing Chesca knew all too well was the occupational hazard of letting nutrition fall to the bottom of the to-do list.

When working cases back to back and traveling across the country at a moment's notice, it was easy to forget to eat right. She had seen it in herself and in others, that a few days of bad eating habits had a way of catching up with a person. Neither she nor Will could afford to have their body act up and slow them down on this hunt. Food was definitely a must.

As they perused the laminated menu looking for

something quick but healthy, Chesca's thoughts drifted to the case in Baton Rouge. She was awaiting more news from the team there to see what puzzle pieces they had, what may have been missed, and she was eager to have another look through their more recent findings to see what she could piece together.

Though it would be a few days, at best, before she could return to those murder scenes, she would if she had to, since she had every intention of making sure she did her best to help solve that case.

"You're always working, aren't you?" Will asked, pulling down Chesca's menu to open the space between them.

Her expression undoubtedly gave a hint of her confusion, but he quickly followed his words with a smile. "I can see it. Your forehead gets a bit scrunchy when you're thinking about work, and right now you look like you're a million miles away."

"Not a million," she said, though slightly embarrassed Will was able to read her so well. "But I guess you're right. Or at least that's what my coworkers accuse me of."

"I'm not saying that's a bad thing," Will laughed. "It shows your commitment to the job, that's for sure. But a little mental break now and then doesn't hurt."

"Like fishing?" Chesca asked, hoping Will would take the lead in piecing together more of his past for her to create a more colorful picture of who he was when not working.

"Any hobby that gives the mind a chance to clear some space is good. Doesn't have to be fishing. Might just be knowing when to enjoy a good cup of coffee and some decent conversation with a new friend."

Chesca folded down her menu and offered Will a direct but amused look. "Friend, huh? You always move this fast?"

His laughter lit up his face and Chesca admired the good nature of her assigned partner. He was right. It was nice to sit back for a moment to think, and give herself a breather. With the benefit of good company, it was pleasurable, and Chesca was grateful he'd made a point of reminding her of that.

"I do what is necessary under the circumstances," Will said slyly. "Like this big to-do your mother recruited me into attending. What's that going to be like?"

"The spring gala?" Chesca cringed at the idea of attending it herself, let alone forcing Will to be there. "You don't have to go, you realize. I doubt there are going to be any security issues to worry about tonight, so if you want—"

With his smooth smile and soft laugh, Will gave Chesca a mischievous look. "What, and miss out on seeing you in that dress again? No way. I'll be there. That is, of course," he said, letting his tone revert back to a more work-related feel, "if we get our share of work done today before this thing starts up. When is that, by the way?"

It was less than convenient, as far as Chesca was

concerned, that her family obligations had to be mixed in with her working plans. The timing was incredible, to show up in Boston and work this case while Abigail Thorne was hosting the Thorne Family Foundation event of the year. "We'll make it when we make it. Work comes first," she said. "Though admittedly my mother would have a fit if we arrived anytime after eight."

"Then we're good. We have lots of time," Will said, checking his watch. "Once we get our bellies full, we'll hit the road and go long."

They ordered clubhouse sandwiches and garden salads, to be quick with their meal but also take in enough veggies to satisfy their health concerns. It was far too easy to rely on cheeseburgers and fries when on the road, and Chesca was pleased to hear Will was equally interested in making sure they got something half decent into their systems.

The one benefit of the evening's social activity, Chesca thought, would be the enormous assortment of food. If there was one thing Abigail Thorne did not skimp on, it was making sure her guests were well fed.

"It's an annual thing?" Will asked, as they dug into their lunch. "So, you're used to doing this party thing all the time, I take it."

Chesca laughed. "Used to and happy to, are very different things, you know. But yes, I am accustomed to making public appearances for my parents' sake at least a couple times per year. However," she said, using her tone to emphasize her meaning, "don't think my life is anything like what you see here. Just because I was raised in it, doesn't mean I am on the socialite express. Heck, I rarely go out, and when I do it's usually something more like this."

"I don't know whether to feel complimented or slapped in the face," Will joked. "But you don't have to explain that to me. I figured that out yesterday, you know. It's easy to see you're a lot more like me in that regard. Family and tradition have their place, but I can see your respect for your parents and commitment to attending such obligatory events is only one small piece of your relationship with them, or of who you are. From what I can tell, you'd have more fun out on the swamps with the likes of me, getting down and dirty. In the mud and rain, I mean."

"I don't know about that," Chesca said, keeping her words friendly. She did like the sound of the life Will had described, but she wasn't sure if agreeing with him when he joked about such things would set her up for something she didn't want to entertain. Though the thought of getting down and dirty with William Evans? It was enough to prompt Chesca to change the topic. "But I do know we have some serious work to do this afternoon."

To the side of the table, Chesca laid out some of the paperwork she'd brought into the restaurant for them to review.

"Workaholic," Will joked, then made a clearing for the papers so it was safe from his coffee cup and saucer. "What more do we got?"

"According to the CIA files, Jackie Cavanaugh died twenty-four years ago."

Chesca watched as Will gave her the reactive expression she was expecting. "Dead, huh? Something tells me you disagree with that."

"You're right. I don't buy it." Chesca flipped through some pages in her personal notebook and shared them with Will. "From what I was told by another Athena graduate, the killer that Salvatore Giambi hired? Had a signature she left behind at her scenes."

It was Bethany James who had shared that information with Chesca over the phone, but Chesca felt no need to use her name as a reference point in the conversation. Not that she didn't trust Will, but she wanted to keep as many names quiet as possible. After all, who was to say if they were being followed—and if any eavesdroppers caught wind of other agents or Athenians, she didn't want to put someone in a position of jeopardy.

"Maybe it wasn't common to think of things such as this back then," Chesca said, thinking out loud about how something like this wouldn't have seemed important decades ago. "But it's more common now to keep an eye out for a signature at the scene of a crime. Every serial has one, spree killers often leave personal markings, you know the drill."

Will stirred some extra ranch dressing onto his salad as he said, "I'm with you. So what's the signature?"

"She left a Queen of Hearts playing card at her scenes,

according to Giambi, when he made his confession to the FBI. At the time, it wouldn't have meant anything."

"But to us, it means something," Will said, catching on to the trend.

"If Giambi's blackmailer was known as the CIA code name Weaver, but left a Queen of Hearts playing card..."

Will finished Chesca's train of thought. "She may also be known as the Queen of Hearts, in other situations."

"There's no way it's coincidence," Chesca said. She finished off the remainder of her club sandwich, and slid the empty plates toward the edge of the table to clear more space. "And the CIA files say Jackie signed all her kills with the same sort of playing card. Which leads me to believe Jackie Cavanaugh has to be Weaver, and she has to be..."

"The Queen of Hearts."

"Precisely."

Will slid a few bills to the waitress and Chesca protested his gesture. "I got it, Will, don't worry about it."

He nodded to the waitress though and shooed off Chesca's offer. "Hey, let me get this one. You're taking care of dinner tonight with that fancy family thing of yours. It's the least I can do."

"Fair enough," she said, not wanting to drag out an argument over the tab. "Listen, according to the CIA files, Jackie Cavanaugh was sent on several missions in Vietnam during the war."

As they left their tip and exited the restaurant to head back out on the road, Chesca continued to download information to Will. "Evidently, several North Vietnamese officers that were killed were credited to her."

They started out the drive to the waterfront with a list of destinations in hand. They aimed to take a direct approach in digging up some additional information as to Jackie's background, and there was no better place than the streets and the neighborhoods Sergeant Waters had suggested to find real-life details that would perhaps shed some insight into how Jackie operated, and perhaps even give a clue as to where she was hiding out these days.

"Seems she had her hands full," Will said, as Chesca outlined some of Jackie's Vietnam activities.

"And, apparently, she was almost killed herself."

"How'd that make the file?"

Chesca sifted through a few paragraphs, intrigued by the information she was privy to. "One of these reports suggests that Jackie was set up by someone for the release of some POWs, so we'll have to look into who that might have been."

Will rolled down the driver side window to let some air into the stuffy vehicle. It had the stale smell of a rental car, and it was too chilly a day to turn on the air conditioning, yet it was warm and moist enough in the car to require some fresh air.

He kept his eyes on the road as he carried on the conversation with Chesca. "Whoever it was might have a few things to say about our girl."

"Exactly. But something else in here is unbelievable."

"What's that?"

"Her handler back in Vietnam was Eric Pace."

Will pulled to the side of the road when their journey was complete, landing them square in the center of gang turf. "I recognize that name. Why?"

"Pace was the former Army Chief of Staff. But you probably know that name for other reasons," Chesca said, shaking her head at what she was beginning to see as a much bigger playing field for Arachne. "He's in prison. Doing time for trying to kill Gabe Monihan."

"The president?"

Chesca nodded her head. "The president. Which means, he won't be going anywhere anytime soon."

Will gave Chesca a knowing look. "That will make it that much easier for us to find him and have a little chat."

"You took the words right out of my mouth."

Chapter 12

"Thanks, Delphi," Chesca said as she made some impromptu arrangements over her cell phone. Though she didn't normally carry on information exchanges over the phone with Oracle business, Chesca knew this had to be settled right away. "We'll turn in the rental car in the morning and catch whatever flight we can to get us there as soon as possible."

"You certainly have connections," Will commented as Chesca closed her cell phone conversation with Delphi. "Good to know we don't have to waste any time getting from A to B."

Now that they were aware of Eric Pace's involvement with Weaver—who Chesca was now certain was also Arachne—she wanted to get them in a meeting with

Pace as soon as possible to see what else she could dig up. Her hopes were that with enough information, they would not only be able to put a trace on Arachne's whereabouts, but also gain enough intelligence to jeopardize any further plans on the sociopath's agenda.

"Doesn't hurt to have friends in high places," Chesca said as she crossed the cobblestone street with Will. They made their way to a lower-level pub Waters suggested they check into for one of the Cavanaugh boys. "And I suppose we're about to see if we have friends in low places too."

Waters had informed them that the youngest Cavanaugh brother had a recent falling-out with the family, and that he was carrying a grudge over a share of funds unequally split between them.

That was the thing with criminals. It never mattered where or how they got their money, so long as they felt they received their fair share of a presumed entitlement. Theft was theft, but being double-crossed by a family member or fellow gang player was a whole other faux pas in the criminal world. It was against their mislaid code of ethics.

Down the narrow stairwell, Chesca and Will took caution as they entered territory unknown to them. While this historic landscape of a formerly quaint Boston neighborhood seemed harmless from a distance, much like what television viewers would have seen in the sitcom series *Cheers,* this was not a place for good times and cheap beer.

The area had yet to undergo a renaissance, and

instead was increasingly infiltrated by underground criminal activities, having been taken over by drug lords and mob business. To get the info they wanted, and ensure their personal safety, Chesca and Will would have to ensure they played with some respect while in the playground where crime rules and the laws of the land don't always apply.

Upon entering the dark basement bar, they were greeted by a rough and oversized bouncer, no doubt packing more than one personal weapon. His height and weight combined presented enough to intimidate a normal passerby, thereby keeping out stragglers and those who had no real business amidst the criminal crowd.

While Chesca knew their abilities in fending off physical attacks, with her background in martial arts and Will's ability to protect army generals, she didn't want to rely on physical capabilities alone. Instead, she used what she knew best, when it came to working people. Her mind.

"We need to talk to Junior," she said, ensuring her vocal pitch presented an even keel to show her ground. Having studied body movements, vocal intonations, and the slightest of tics in her pursuit to understand human behavior and criminal interaction, she was also able to use that know-how to her advantage, aiming to best present herself however a situation called for her to behave.

In many ways, it was the same chameleon ability she called upon when attending formal family functions at the Thorne mansion, and in spending social time with those associated with her parents. No matter the circumstance, Chesca was able to blend in and mimic those in her company.

"I don't think so," the overgrown bouncer growled.

Chesca offered a coy smile to the man. "I disagree. See, I have a feeling Junior's gotten himself hooked up with some bad business as of late," Chesca said, using the information Sergeant Waters had shared with her. Thinking she might need some leverage in gaining access to a mob son, she had made sure to rifle through the files of what the Cavanaugh boys had been up to, what she might be able to use as a bargaining tool. She was now thankful she had gone to such trouble.

"You're not getting through, lady," the man said.

"You tell Junior, my friend and I are going to wait outside and if he feels like chatting, I happen to know a very nice sergeant who would be happy to lessen a charge or two that's going to save him both time and money."

Without even waiting for an answer, Chesca guided Will back up the stairs to wait outside, praying her bait would work.

She had discussed it briefly with Waters to see what sort of deals she could work out if need be, and with Junior and Sonny, she knew she'd have a handful of ammunition to work with.

She wasn't going to freely hand out promises she couldn't keep, nor was she going to be overly generous. But when the time came for it, Chesca knew she could make equal trades to encourage the sharing of information, if that's what it took.

When they made it outside, Chesca took a seat on the bottom step of a neighboring flower shop. She knew it wouldn't take long if Junior was going to give her an earful. If he didn't come out within a few minutes, it would mean her game had failed.

"What do you make of that," Will began, then rolled his eyes in the direction of the opposite side of the street. "I wouldn't look directly, but if you ask me it seems there's a sitting duck keeping an eye on old Junior's bar here, don't you think?"

Chesca took Will's suggestion and casually let her eyes roam across the cobblestone side street, taking her time to let her peripheral vision pick up the presence of a lone figure, sitting in a parked car down an alleyway, and holding up the guise of reading a newspaper.

"Seems Junior may be a popular guy," Chesca said, getting the same negative vibe her partner no doubt shared.

It was a busy street, so there was a remote possibility the man was in fact waiting for someone to come out of a neighborhood store. But the evidence suggested otherwise. Whoever he was, he was on the lookout.

Outside the burgundy sedan, Chesca could see there was a pile of cigarette butts. The man had been sitting there some time and had carelessly dumped them out of his car's ashtray. From the pile of them, she figured he had been there a few hours, and she wondered if perhaps it was his daily post to sit in that location and monitor the traffic coming in and out of the bar.

Only thing she couldn't make out for certain was

whether he was working for Junior, or was hired by someone else to keep an eye on the Cavanaugh brother. One thing she knew for sure, was it was definitely not an unmarked police car. It didn't fit the mold.

"Interesting," Chesca said, then caught herself apologizing to a young man who nearly tripped over her feet as he passed by them sitting on the narrow sidewalk. The boy kept walking, and Chesca was perturbed that he had carelessly dropped litter on the street, especially given that there was a garbage container located just a few feet down.

But then, Chesca noticed something that caught her attention.

She got up from her step, and cleared her throat to cue Will to follow her lead. She picked up the disposed coffee cup left by the man on the street, and walked to the garbage container with Will by her side, then disposed of the cup.

"Feeling like a good citizen?" Will asked, likely wondering what it was that prompted Chesca to leave their place in waiting for news from Junior.

"Nope," she said, keeping up the pace in her walk. "That coffee cup? Had a piece of paper rolled up in it. Evidently, Junior knows his place is being staked out by someone, because he certainly doesn't want to come out into the broad daylight to chat with us. But the good news is, he's going to talk."

"Where are we going?"

"O'Brien's Deli," Chesca said, relaying the brief instructions Junior's messenger had shared with them in the coffee cup note. "Just around the corner. I'm guessing he's taking a back entrance to get out from the bar to meet us there. Smart guy."

"For making a deal?"

Chesca nodded and smiled at Will. "And for knowing how to keep his movements low-key."

Will cleared his throat and Chesca waited as she wondered what it was that Will was hesitating to say.

"You sure that guy in the car was keeping an eye on Junior?" he asked, finally.

"I'd assume as such, wouldn't you?"

He shrugged his shoulders. "For now, I'd rather assume nothing. Especially on account of your recent car problems and the hotel being turned inside out. Who knows who has been tracking your movements, Chesca. Better safe than sorry, know what I'm saying?"

Of course that was an option Chesca had already considered. With the unwelcoming committee she had already experienced in her short time back in Boston, she knew full well someone could be trailing her movements.

After all, someone had known to make a point with her rental car, and that was after she'd barely arrived in the city. And the hotel? Someone knew where she was staying. Sure, Will could be right. For all she knew, someone could have been watching their every step, waiting for an opportune time to introduce themselves.

"We'll be careful," Chesca said to Will, as she wanted him to know she too understood how a few close contacts could imply more trouble was on the way.

Nothing worth knowing came without its price, she knew, so regardless of how prepared she and Will felt, it was still in their best interest to keep an active guard.

"This is the deli?" Will asked, as Chesca led him across the street to a corner countertop grill that looked like it had been transported from the fifties.

O'Brien's had been a part of this neighborhood for as long as Chesca could remember. Though this was definitely not the area of Boston she hung out in as a youngster, she'd known of the establishment's existence from the many times it had made the evening news. Between beer brawls that ended up in the middle of the street or late-night shootings, O'Brien's was known around the 'hood as a rough-and-tumble kind of bar not recommended for the faint of heart.

Though from the outside, she could sense why it was also a popular eatery for the locals. The smell of beer-soaked roasted slices of beef wafted through the damp spring air, and though they had just eaten, Chesca felt her stomach warm up to the idea of something sinful to snack on.

The thought faded quickly, though, as they entered the deli and took a seat in a back corner booth. Will slid in the seat beside Chesca so they could both keep an eye on the door for their person of interest.

It was only a moment before a stout, unshaven man approached them from behind and took a seat opposite them.

He was older than Chesca had imagined, though she

reminded herself of the timeline of when the Cavanaugh brothers were at their peak in criminal activities. The work had obviously done a number on his facade, with his skin worn like leather, and he likely appeared older than he was.

At any rate, Chesca realized Junior's name was neither a reflection of his age, nor his size, as the aged, large-framed man made himself comfortable.

Immediately, she picked up a nervous tic he had, his right eye flinching at the slightest sound. And his hands were constantly occupied, drumming the top of the melamine table, in no particular rhythm.

"I'm listening," Junior said, cracking his neck, and shifting his slouched posture. "What is it you think you can do for me?"

"It depends," Chesca said, making deliberate eye contact with the youngest of the Cavanaugh boys. "On what you can do for me. I'm only making a deal if it's fair."

"Fair ain't got nothing to do with it," he said, clearly angered at the notion he was wasting his time.

Chesca laid it out for him rather quickly. Like Junior, she didn't want to waste her time either. "With me it does. But if you can help us out in any way, I'll be sure to talk to the cops and get something suitable for you, in exchange for your cooperation. How's that?"

He scoffed for a moment, shaking his head. "Yeah, that shit always sounds better up front than in reality. But go on, what do you want to know?"

Chesca gave a basic rundown of what she wanted to

know about Junior's sister Jackie, though she spared him the details about why she wanted to know and for whom she was working.

"It's pretty simple, Junior," she said as a matter of fact. "Your sister has a reputation but I need some validity to back up what I've been hearing."

The youngest of the mob family sipped at his draft beer. The bartender sent over a round of drinks on the house, and Chesca guessed Jackie wasn't the only Cavanaugh to have a mean reputation.

"It's about right," Junior said, carrying on with his finger drumming. The sound would be enough to drive Chesca batty had she not honed the skill of learning how to drown out white noise. "Jackie's been a nut job for as long as I can remember. Even when she was a kid she had a screw loose. Bitch."

Chesca noticed while she paid all her attention to the disclosure of information from Junior, Will was occupying his time by doing his job. His eyes continually scanned the deli in a casual way so as to pick up anything out of the ordinary. She was pleased to see him do his part of the job in keeping an eye out on their behalf, but she was thankful he didn't feel the need to barge in on her investigation.

"She always thought she was top shit, bossing us around when we were kids. Thinking because she was the oldest she had a say in how everything would work in the family," Junior went on. Though he and his brothers were in their fifties, Arachne was the senior of the group, and clearly felt her age difference was enough merit to call the shots.

"What happened when she went to Vietnam?"

Chesca needed to make more of a connection to Jackie serving overseas so she could tie pieces together that would confirm that Jackie was in fact the CIA operative known as Weaver. She was hoping Junior could shed more light on the subject with some personal background information.

"Ah, hell, she ain't never talked about that with any of us," he said to Chesca's disappointment. "But I can tell you one thing. She was messed up long before she went there. I know when she was there she had some weird inner fight going on, 'cuz the woman talks in her sleep. I picked up on something or other, but as far as I'm concerned she was damaged goods forever ago."

"How's that?"

Chesca didn't want to leave the deli empty-handed. She needed to know more of Jackie's personality and her psyche if she was going to be able to decode more about how her chemical makeup dictated her behavior.

"She doesn't take it well when things happen outside of her control, ya know? Like when each of our folks died, God rest their souls," Junior said, crossing his chest. "Of course it was bad to go through, but Jackie? Shit, she couldn't handle it, took it real bad. She was already messed up in the head from my view, but that pushed her over the edge, ya know. She went all whacko and shit, never really accepting it. But hey, life happens."

"Junior," Chesca said, taking the conversation in a new direction, hoping for the best. She was headed into dangerous territory, but with Will by her side and Junior's candid nature, she felt ready to dig deeper. "What about the gangs. Jackie ever get involved in any of it?"

He nodded to the bartender to receive another round of draft beer, then chugged the remaining liquid from his current glass. "Hell yeah, you kidding me? But hey, I gotta give her credit. She never got into the drugs and stuff, so at least she tried to keep it clean."

"But she was involved in some of the more," Chesca thought for a moment before continuing, "negotiating tactics of the business?"

"You got that right. And hell, she was in some ways a mixed blessing. On one hand the chick would fly off the handle with one of us for no good reason. But the one good thing about her was she had no problem taking someone out on the town, if you get what I'm saying."

"I think I have an idea," Chesca said, imagining his older sister handling some of the bad deals in town. Knowing what she was capable of, it didn't take much to imagine how Jackie Cavanaugh could settle the score for an unpaid debt or drug deal gone wrong.

As Junior recounted his youth shared with his siblings in the mob circuit, Chesca noted how lax he was about what his sister had been up to. Nothing seemed to affect him in any way, regarding her role in the criminal underground, and any time he mentioned Jackie's name his hands would hit the counter again, drumming off tension.

"I have to ask," Chesca said, wanting to know something she could definitely work with in locating Arachne. "When was the last time you saw her? Do you know where she's at by any chance?"

As Junior accepted his fresh draft of beer, he laughed in Chesca's direction. "Hell, it's been so many years I couldn't even tell you. That woman's a ghost. No one's seen her around in some time, and I got to be honest with you, it's like she doesn't even exist anymore. I suspect she's dead."

Though she refused to believe it to be true, Chesca nudged Will when she heard those words.

"I was afraid you might say that."

Chapter 13

The sun had begun to fade into the evening as Will and Chesca made their way back to the Thorne mansion. The spring fling fund-raising gala hosted by Abigail Thorne would soon be underway and Chesca wanted to arrive on time.

For the return trip back to the overpriced neighborhood, Chesca took control of the driver's seat of the rental car, as Will had received a phone call on his cell phone just as they were about to head out.

It was his great-aunt Christine Evans and he wanted to be sure to have a moment to catch up with her and assure her that everything was in progress.

"Tomorrow we're flying out of Boston," he explained

to her about the change in investigative destinations. "Francesca has a meeting set up with Eric Pace."

Chesca did her best to extend the courtesy of listening in as little as possible to Will's conversation. Though it was hard to ignore and technically it was mostly pertaining to her assignment, she also wanted to be courteous in letting him have his personal space.

She tried to focus on the new information she'd received regarding Jackie's background, courtesy of her brother Junior. Though he wasn't able to point them in any specific direction, it was solid background information she could use in assembling a profile on the serial blackmailer.

Now that she was gathering an idea of what sort of life events motivated Jackie, and which ones she'd reacted to poorly, she could begin to diagnose Jackie's psyche and aim to predict as much movement on her part as possible.

What was bothering Chesca, however, was the notion that Junior had, though slightly jokingly, commented on his theory that Jackie may in fact be dead. That, combined with the CIA files suggesting it as truth, worried Chesca.

She knew in her gut that it wasn't true.

From what her instinct was telling her, Jackie just felt like Arachne, and with the information about her alias Weaver signing kills with the Queen of Hearts playing card, it was too much to ignore.

What Chesca really wanted to know, though, was

how the CIA managed to declare her case files closed, and presume her death was real. Could it be, Chesca wondered, that Jackie Cavanaugh was still active with the agency, and had somehow made a deal to keep her identity secret and her whereabouts unknown?

"The weather is fine, I packed for it, so don't you worry," Will said to Christine. Chesca listened as he spoke to his great-aunt with warmth. The tone he used was one of friendliness and respect, and she herself longed for that kind of family connection.

She did have relationships close to that, with the women she came to know and respect at Athena Academy. They were her family in every way, Chesca believed. But from time to time she longed for the kind of home life she knew was possible, but just wasn't able to develop with her own kin.

Not that she didn't try. Of course, to Will or anyone else, it likely came off that Chesca was short with her parents, perhaps lacked polite respect, and held on tight to tensions that were hard to understand. But that was now.

Time and time again, Chesca had tried, as a young girl then again as a young woman, to bond with her mother and father, but it was to no avail. They weren't willing to cooperate, and it took more than one person to carry on a healthy and successful relationship.

"Chesca?" Will said, passing the cell phone to her. The look in his eyes was one of warmth, so she suspected Christine just wanted reassurance. "Christine wants to speak with you."

"How are you?" Chesca asked as she accepted the call from Christine Evans.

"Very well, thank you. Francesca," Christine said, taking on a quiet, contemplative tone. "Will tells me you're off to see Eric Pace."

"That's right."

"Then let me brief you on what kind of man he is so you know what to expect."

Chesca listened attentively while keeping her eyes on the road ahead. They were still a half hour away from the Thorne home, but it was important to Chesca that she absorb as much information on Pace as possible so that she could feel prepared for their departure the next day. She knew she was lucky in having the ability to meet with Pace on such short notice, with his prison term being well underway. But, thankfully, Delphi had made sure to set up the appropriate connections.

"Not only was he in Vietnam," Christine explained to Chesca. "But he also had command in the Gulf War, so he's military through and through. And don't think he doesn't have the ego and attitude to go along with it."

"Good to know," Chesca said, taking in the information from someone who would have known more of Pace's personal demeanor and how it played a hand in how he operated.

Though she didn't generally buy into stereotypes about roles people adopted, it was handy to hear about Pace letting his position in the army get a grasp on his attitude. Chesca knew many a good man and woman who had served time in high-ranking positions for the military who were perfectly capable of dealing with others in a respectful manner. But she'd also met a person or two who enjoyed a power trip a bit too much for their own good. Clearly, this was the case with Eric Pace.

Christine continued to share her knowledge of the man. "He has a pretty good chip on his shoulder and can be downright nasty when he wants to be, so keep your guard up, Francesca. He's the kind of man who can and will do anything to keep his country in good shape, but he has a different code of ethics than you and me. What makes sense to him may not be reasonable to the average person."

Drawing on her knowledge of the terrible incidents that had occurred over the past few years at Athena Academy, Christine also relayed to Chesca some information regarding Pace's knowledge of Lab 33.

Though Chesca knew only the basics as far as what Lab 33 had meant to Athena Academy, she had kept abreast of the highly sensitive activities being conducted there as conversations had swirled around her alumnus both through the Web site and in personal connections.

It was more than twenty-five years ago that someone named Aldrich Peters had worked on some questionable science, by genetically manipulating human eggs. The eggs were provided by Arachne, and she'd hired surrogates to bear her three children Kwan-Sook, Lilith and Echo.

It was only a few years ago that it became known that those three children possessed genetic enhancements that provided them with exceptional abilities.

Just under two years ago, Chesca became aware of the trouble with Lab 33 when it was busted by authorities with the assistance of Athena grads. Not long after that, the lab was destroyed, and from what Christine was telling Chesca, Eric Pace was aware of the entire lab operations, from the get-go.

"He's a schemer, Francesca. He's been known to take out anyone who gets in the way of his agenda, political or otherwise."

Chesca was already aware that Pace was Jackie Cavanaugh's handler during Vietnam, and as Chesca listened to Christine tell her about Pace's personal views, she could hardly believe the power such a person had.

Evidently, Pace believed that the Bay of Pigs was a necessity and that Cuba had far worse coming, suggesting that the military should have dropped snakes overhead in an effort to oust Castro.

"Thank you, Christine. I appreciate the information," Chesca said. She was grateful to have insider info to prepare her for the interview with Pace. "We'll do our best."

"How are you finding it, working with Will? Is everything okay between the two of you?"

Chesca didn't know how to respond to that. Of course things were going fine. Will had been a blessing despite her initial protest that she didn't need a bodyguard to trail her every move. And, quite honestly, Chesca was happy to have the company. Will had proven to be an interesting character with a great sense of humor, and a serious side he applied to work. In many ways, she couldn't have asked for a better partner.

"Yes, thank you, everything is fine in that regard," Chesca said, not sure she wanted Will to know she was talking about him to his aunt. Though she was fond of his company, she didn't want him thinking she was overly pleased with his presence. But she knew her blush had returned, and hoped to hell he didn't put two and two together.

"Good. Then I'll expect to hear some good results from your teamwork."

"Absolutely," Chesca said, then handed the phone back to Will so he could say his goodbyes.

As she drove the final few miles to her parents' home, Chesca thought of how much she appreciated that call from Christine. Though she realized it was likely to ensure her great-nephew was satisfied and business was in order, it also gave Chesca a chance to hear from a mentor, and take pride in the people she had come to know through the Academy.

Christine Evans was an amazing woman, this much Chesca knew. As an ex-army officer who held her own in the call to duty, she was able to conduct business on a professional level and enforce her convictions with grace and dignity while still making a point. But she could also blend easily with any sort of demographic, and she never took too much unhealthy pride in her role in society. Instead, her contributions to the school and to the community were made in a quiet manner, showing her modesty in all she was able to offer to the young women of Athena Academy and many others she chose to support in alternative means.

Chesca appreciated how hands-on Christine was with her students, and to this day she found it easy to carry on a level conversation with her. Not many students of elite academic institutions could say that they had such a personal relationship with their principal. Many of them wouldn't be able to claim any association whatsoever to a higher-up. But Christine Evans was personable, well-loved and intent on carrying on the dream of Athena Academy that she and her friend Marion Gracelyn had shared for so many years. It was her loyalty to her friends and to her society that undoubtedly propelled her to continue on with her personal conviction.

"She's very fond of you," Will said, after he hung up the phone with his great-aunt.

"You think?"

Though Chesca was certainly pleased to be in association with Christine, she hadn't really given much thought to how the woman viewed her. She merely assumed she treated all Athena graduates with the same courtesy and friendliness. Christine didn't play favorites, this much Chesca knew.

"I know for a fact. She told me."

The smile on Will's face indicated that he knew more than he was letting on, but Chesca wasn't going to take the bait to inquire further. She was just pleased and proud to have somehow made an impression on someone of Christine's standing.

"It's nice to hear," Chesca opted to say. "I'll take the compliment with grace."

"You should. Because it's true, and I agree with my aunt. You're an interesting person, Francesca Thorne."

As she kept her focus on the road ahead, Chesca tried to use her peripheral vision to scan Will's face. Was he being sincere or jabbing her with a joke? But from what she could tell, he was extending a genuine compliment to her, and she wasn't sure whether to change the topic or accept the sentiment with a return compliment.

But Will didn't wait for her to make up her mind. "You don't know what to say to that, do you?"

Chesca smiled. He was getting to know her well, really quickly. "You got me. When it comes to compliments," she said, "I'm afraid I have a hard time accepting them generally. Goes back to hearing them fall out of my mother's mouth, only to be followed with a 'but' or a reprimand. There always seemed to be a catch."

"But I'm sure you've been complimented by many people. You're a stunning woman, and I can bet you had a lot of guys trying to get to know you. If I know men, they don't hold back on giving compliments to beautiful women."

Again Chesca was taken aback by his attention, and this time she could not hide the warmth and color rising in her cheeks.

"Wow, knock me out while I'm down, why don't

you," she joked, then decided to share some personal pieces of her own history with Will as they rounded out the drive home. "But to clarify, just because the boys were after me, didn't mean their compliments were sincere. Again, always seemed to be a catch, one way or the other."

Will's voice took on an intrigued tone. "No luck with men then, is that what you're telling me?"

He didn't know the half of it, and Chesca was certain she didn't want to get into too many details of her disastrous—and nonexistent—love life.

"Something like that. Guess it just hasn't been in the cards for me. Somehow I thought it would be different once I got away from the Thorne family matchmaking service my mother subjected me to, but I guess it just hasn't been the right time or the right person." Chesca was embarrassed at how easily she talked to Will about her personal life. She immediately felt the need to get off topic. "But it doesn't matter. I am happy with my work. I love the thrill of the hunt, the chase, the adrenaline rush."

She trailed off into another direction, but Will sat up straight in his seat and took newfound interest in the rear window. "I hope that's true," he said. "Because you'll want to remember that when your adrenaline kicks it up a notch in a minute."

Following his line of sight, Chesca found a focal point within the rearview mirror and knew right away what Will was referring to.

"How long, do you think?" Chesca asked, when she realized they were being followed by a car that looked a lot like the burgundy sedan that had been sitting outside Junior's bar.

"I just noticed him a minute ago," Will said, adjusting in his seat. "But he's being smart about maintaining enough distance. Had we not spotted him at the bar, there's no way we'd pick up on being followed."

She checked her speed. Noticed she was driving at a reasonable pace on the single-lane road leading to the high-end neighborhood where her parents lived. Along here, she knew the roads well and could get off the road and away from their tail if she wanted to. But she wasn't sure they wanted to lose their trailer just yet. Her curiosity had her wondering who that man was and who he worked for.

As Will had suggested earlier, there was a possibility that whoever was on Chesca's tail might indeed still be following them. Yet there had been no movements made throughout the day, and Chesca was beginning to wonder if perhaps it was someone working for the Cavanaugh family who was parked in that alleyway and was now behind them on the road.

"It's best we take them off the beaten path," Will suggested. "Unless you want to lead whoever that is straight to your family's home."

Chesca had already considered that. Although they were a few minutes from the Thorne mansion, she didn't have any intention of ruining her mother's annual fund-raiser by hightailing it into the property with a pursuit in progress.

She took Will's advice and turned down a side road she knew from her younger days. The path led from the main road alongside the river, down to some private property that was meant to be a golf course but the residents surrounding the area had voted to keep it as a green space, worried they wouldn't be able to control the membership of yet another club.

As suspected, the burgundy sedan turned behind them, and began to pick up speed.

Though she had no need to use it thus far on this case, she asked Will to reach into the backseat to grab her personal gun, as a precaution.

"You know where you're headed?" he asked, keeping his eyes focused on the reflection of the car behind them.

"The road does a U-turn down by the water, and there's a path that cuts through that I'll turn into, and hopefully lose him for long enough to spring back out on him from the opposite direction."

She did as she outlined, cutting through some green space and taking a graveled and unused side path, quickly picking up the pace to outrun the other car for a moment.

As she turned off the lights of the car, they watched their follower pass by at an increased speed, and Chesca put her foot back on the gas to head in the direction where she hoped she would be able to cut him off.

As they made their attempts to cut the guy short,

Will made a quick call to Sergeant Waters, requesting he send appropriate cars to the scene.

Earlier, the sergeant had reminded them that he was at their disposal if they ran into any complications with the Cavanaugh mob, and both Chesca and Will suspected that was exactly what they had encountered out here on the back road.

He gave the closest intersection as a reference point and described the area Chesca had driven into. But as Chesca rounded the corner to where they had hoped to find the man who was following them, they were caught by surprise.

The burgundy car was there, but not in a way that they had hoped to find it.

"I don't believe it," Chesca said, as she shared the same vision Will did, and he filled in the gaps for his conversation to the police department.

"You're also going to want to send the fire department," Will said to Sergeant Waters. "Because that car is burning up in flames."

Chapter 14

"I'm beginning to think you're on a streak of bad luck," Sergeant Waters said to Chesca upon his arrival.

"That's an understatement," she replied, wanting to get down to the matter at hand and sort out who was in the burgundy sedan that had been following them. "Your men come across anyone yet?"

Waters shook his head negatively. "Nope. But he couldn't have gotten far."

As soon as the convoy of emergency vehicles arrived at the scene, a handful of uniformed officers began to scope out the area looking for their guy. It was immediately evident the driver had fled the vehicle, but whether that was before the car burst into flames, or after, was yet to be determined.

At this point, they were still trying to figure out how the car sparked up, and whether the fire was set by the driver or if it had occurred without his knowledge.

"I've run the plates," Waters said to Chesca and Will, as they walked alongside the gravel pathway, keeping an eye out for the wanted man. "And nothing has come up to give any indication that this car is associated with the Cavanaughs."

Will shook his head, and for the first time since she'd met him, Chesca could see he was annoyed with the turn of unfortunate events. Evidently, he was starting to get agitated with the way things were progressing, despite not knowing who was after them.

Chesca knew it must be frustrating for him, as a bodyguard watching for those out to sabotage her goal, but lacking the knowledge of who in particular he had to keep his eyes on. It meant everyone was a threat, and that made his job harder.

"It was parked in the alleyway across from Junior's," Will said to Waters, and he continued to share what he'd witnessed at the time. "Francesca noticed how long he had been sitting there due to the amount of cigarette butts he had dumped outside his door. Whoever he is, he knew to expect us."

But if Waters was correct, Chesca thought, that man might not have had anything to do with the Cavanaughs. And if that was the case, he may have been after Chesca. Not knowing who he was or for whom he worked posed a few obstacles in figuring out their next steps.

"He's out here somewhere," Waters said with conviction in his voice and an angered expression on his face. Like Chesca and Will, he was showing determination in wanting to put an end to this cat-and-mouse hunt. "Nobody runs from a burning car and gets too far too quick, even if he jumped and ran."

It had only been a minute while Chesca and Will ducked their car out from the main path to wait for the trailer's car to pass. If the fire had been set intentionally, Chesca realized it meant the man would have been willing and able to do such a thing at the drop of a hat.

Who could plan to blow up their own car within moments, and who would want to?

While Waters had suggested the incident didn't have an immediate connection to the Cavanaugh mob, Chesca couldn't help but think of the close calls other investigations had endured at the hands of Arachne and her employees.

Beth had warned her of such a thing earlier, telling Chesca how Giambi's helicopter had exploded right after it took off, without him in it, giving him a narrow escape. Her own rental car had already been tampered with upon her arrival to Boston. There had to be something that would make sense of this.

"Best I can do," Waters offered, "is to keep you informed as to what evidence we find out here, what else we can put together based on the car's make and model, and then share that as it comes in."

Chesca was grateful for the offer. "It may not seem

like much to go on right now, but that would be great. You have my number. Call it anytime."

If there had been no other pressing matters for Chesca to tend to, she would perhaps have opted to stay in Boston while the investigation was underway so she could receive the information in person. But with the interview set up with Eric Pace for the next day, Chesca didn't want to leave it to chance that they'd find more information here.

She knew when she had a lead attached to a live, breathing person to get that in order right away. People change their minds about having something to say, leave the country, or even die, and she didn't want to risk the chance of losing out on her one-on-one with Eric Pace. He would potentially be a great resource to Chesca in learning more about Arachne.

The evidence from the car would provide a potential lead into who was after Chesca, but her own personal safety was not at the top of her priorities right now. She knew she could make it through rough situations, and it wasn't anything new to her to be someone's prey.

But talking with Eric Pace had to come first, as did putting together the puzzle pieces on finding the Queen of Hearts, also known as Arachne.

"You better be able to make yourself presentable very soon, young lady," Abigail Thorne said, scolding her daughter.

Knowing how late they were, and the informal attire

they were wearing was less than decent at that point in the day, they had opted to sneak in the back staff entrance to avoid making a scene that would send Chesca's mother into a complete coronary. But when Abigail Thorne got wind that her daughter and partner had arrived back at the house, it didn't take long for her to hunt them down and give them a piece of her mind.

"The guests have begun to arrive and the cocktail bar is open. Don't you dare make a mockery of this event," she warned with a look directed at both Will and Chesca.

"We'll only be a moment," Chesca said, knowing it wouldn't take her long to get ready. She wasn't one to spend hours in front of the mirror, and thankfully her short hair ensured that a quick shower and shampoo would be all she would need to meet her mother's expectations.

Long ago, she knew her mother had given up on seeing Chesca fall in line with the family history of primping, priming and pimping off kin to other rich families. While it used to bother Chesca that she was somehow made to feel like a second-best offspring, she no longer had the time on her hands to give such opinions much time or consideration.

She was who she was, and when her mother seemed to have enough of it, she knew it was the end of her stay at the Thorne mansion.

Abigail gave them each a doubtful once-over before exiting the staff kitchen. "Then get going. I'll be expecting you out front soon. You have responsibilities, Francesca."

Chesca bit her lip. She wanted to mimic her mother's statement, but she realized falling into the role of disobedient child would only fuel her mother's irritation and lower her to the level Abigail expected.

Within thirty minutes, however, Chesca was able to walk out of her old bedroom and meet Will in the hallway so they could make an entrance together. As suspected, she was quick at making the transition in her appearance, and she was also quite pleased to see how well her partner had been able to clean up with just a quick shower and change of clothes.

"You look dapper," she said, though she wanted to say more when she saw how handsome he looked in the finely tailored suit Roger had fitted for him earlier.

She was stunned with how urban and sophisticated the good old boy from the South appeared to her, and though she didn't say much about it, she knew her smile gave away some of her thoughts.

"You're not too bad yourself," he said, eyeing her in the dress he had admired earlier that morning. "Go on, give me a twirl. I want to see this from all angles."

"You're serious."

Will's expression said his request was an earnest one, and though she was embarrassed by his desire to see her spin around, she obliged, laughing while she did so.

"I approve," he said, smiling as she stopped to face him again.

"In that case, shall we?"

Will looped his arm through Chesca's as he escorted

her down the stairwell and they walked through the foyer to join the party in progress.

The Thorne mansion had a large room meant for social events such as this, and was capable of hosting close to two hundred people. It was a large entertaining room, with little furnishing taking up space in the vast formal venue. Off to the east side was a patio lounge that matched the length of the ballroom, and there were several bar stations set up for occasions such as this.

Growing up, Chesca wasn't allowed to use this room as a playroom, though whenever her parents traveled, the nanny let her secretly use the room as a roller-skating rink. To this day, Chesca had never shared that secret with anyone, knowing if it managed to get back to her mother, there would be a steep price to pay, even at her adult age.

The most enjoyable aspect of the evening for Chesca was in watching Will immerse himself in this blue-blood environment. She knew from past experience, it could be overwhelming to bring newcomers into this strange social realm, but there was something joyful about watching Will make himself comfortable amidst some of the area's heftiest millionaires.

She knew, of course, he came from a very respectable family, but there was a difference between the Evanses and the Thornes. Christine Evans and her family of army lifers were neither braggarts nor phonies in their efforts, whereas Chesca believed there was always a distinct aroma of bullshit around the Thorne family homestead.

Chesca had nothing against her family having money. It was in how they showed it off, puffing up their feathers as though they were of a higher class than others, equating better off with better people. And she didn't buy into that way of thinking herself. She instead preferred modesty, knowing well enough not to look a gift horse in the mouth, but also not to allow the horse to make an ass out of herself.

"It's very…shiny," Will said, finally as he scoped out the room's décor. "Is it always this way?"

"Yes and no," Chesca explained. "Obviously, on account of the size of the room the only activities conducted in here are the big social events. And it always looks quite formal. But for the annual spring gala, my mother kicks it up a notch. She likely had a month's worth of work put into it to make it so shiny, as you put it."

It was a black-tie affair. Which meant for each surface, every nook and cranny, a collection of decorating goods had been used in black, white and silver. At least Chesca was grateful Abigail Thorne didn't go over the top with bouquets of highly potent floral arrangements.

While there were several flower groupings throughout the vast room, they were subtle in scent so as not to compete with the aroma of foods being served.

The two of them waded through gatherings of people all busy with small talk, discussing politics, stocks and various investments, and the social gossip of the day.

Chesca knew at some point she would be obliged to make polite conversation with a handful of people her mother would insist she chat with, but she hoped to buy some time before having to do so. For now, she just wanted to scan the room with Will and get him acquainted with the landscape.

It was important to her that he felt welcome and at home. She wasn't sure why, exactly. Perhaps it was that any impressions he assembled from the Thorne event he might naturally associate with Chesca.

As much as her mother made sure everyone knew her daughter was definitely not falling in line with her carefully laid footsteps, Chesca did all she could to prove how unlike her parents she was. Thinking on that, Chesca laughed to herself, realizing she did in fact have something in common with her parents. Their determination to protect their views of how they were perceived by others.

Once she and Will had scouted the room to see what all the dining options were for the evening, they took a moment to peruse the silent auction Abigail Thorne had set up as part of the fund-raiser.

Each year, a group of community volunteers were recruited by the foundation to request items from local businesses and service providers that Abigail could have as prizes for a raffle or silent auction. While the bulk of the income generated from the fund-raiser came from checks being quietly signed in advance of the event, this little addition generated a substantial amount of funds, and also usually added interactive fun for the guests.

No matter what items were up for auction, it was

inevitable that each year there would be a tug of war over at least one prime choice, and by the end of the night the entire crowd would gather to watch the bids rise and rise, to the point of a competition between two opponents.

It could get pretty rowdy, with one person trying to outdo the other in terms of showing who could afford more, but it was also a great source of entertainment for the remainder of the guests. One year, Chesca recalled, a gambling friend of her father's even initiated a pool to wager who could predict the winner of the silent auction. It truly got outrageous and was regarded as one of the highlights of the evening.

For this particular year, Chesca and Will took in the vast variety of expensive items only the guests in attendance would consider a bargain. Yachts. Summer homes. Luxury cars. Diamonds and pearl collections.

Though there was always a handful of lesser priced items, still outside of Chesca's price range, meant for those guests who wanted to bid on an assortment of things, while still contributing to the overall pot.

"Anything you like?" Will asked Chesca as they rounded the end of the corner display table.

"Like versus want?" she joked, knowing fully well she would not be bidding on anything herself, and she suspected Will was a bit out of his realm with the increasing bids as well. "There are some interesting things. Hopefully my mother reaches her goal tonight with the bids. But there won't be anything I want to take home."

"It's all out of my league," Will said, nodding in the direction of services offered by a law office for a one-year retainer. "People actually bid on all these things?"

"Each and every one. And they all get more than they're worth. But that's the point. People don't come here to make a deal. They come to show their support for the event and outplay the others in waving around their big fat checkbooks."

As Chesca finished giving her views on the guests of the fund-raiser, Abigail Thorne interrupted their walk. "It's those checkbooks that keep this foundation in top shape. You do realize, Francesca, these people actually care for the causes they contribute to."

"Yes, I know, Mother. Everyone here is a philanthropist and I shouldn't hold it against any of them if they take a bit too much pride in their pocketbook."

"Never you mind," Abigail said, keeping her tone quiet and words short, so as to ensure privacy in the conversation. "Just make yourself known, and please, promise me you'll be on your best behavior."

"Of course, you have my word," Chesca said, though her mother didn't wait for a reply. Obviously she had given Chesca no choice, but it didn't matter. Other than sharing her personal views with Will, she knew better than to cause a scene by disagreeing with any of the guests or overextending her welcome into any conversation pertaining to money.

"Shall we dance?"

Chesca looked at Will in surprised. "Will, we don't

have to. My mother was just being her usual self. Don't let her intimidate you. We can relax."

"I wasn't thinking of your mother," he said as he led her by the hand to the center of the dance floor. "I was thinking about how amazing you look in that dress and I want to make sure everyone else knows that too. Come on, dance with me. Pretend you're here to have a good time."

The thought hadn't even occurred to Chesca. Have a good time? Until now, she had considered her presence at this event as she had always considered her attendance at the mandatory family functions. Mandatory. It didn't even register with her that she might enjoy herself in the process.

It was hard to imagine having an evening dedicated solely to pleasure when they had so much work to do. She had to figure out how to locate Arachne. They had the meeting with Eric Pace to prepare for. There was someone burning up cars and following their every move. And she also had the case in Baton Rouge to think about.

Amidst all that, was it still possible to enjoy some social time at the spring gala?

"You really need to stop doing that," Will said, brushing Chesca's side and wrapping his hand firmly around her waist.

It was an unusual feeling for her to experience, having not felt the warmth of a man's hand against her body in far too many years.

"Doing what?" she asked, following his lead onto the dance floor.

"Thinking about work. I can tell, you know. Your brow is scrunching up again."

He reached a finger up to her forehead to point to the area he was referring to. His simple touch was enough to cause goose bumps down Chesca's back.

"How is it you think you know me so well, Mr. Evans?" Chesca said, not hiding the flirtatious tone that came naturally from her mouth.

Perhaps it was the ambiance. Or maybe it was the well-paced waltz holding the two of them together. But Chesca was feeling at ease with Will, and she was enjoying the feeling that was stirring within her, despite not knowing how to accept it.

"Must be my sixth sense. That, and I can recognize a bit of my own working mind-set in you. But it's attractive. I like a woman with so much drive for what she does. You enjoy your work, and I enjoy watching you work."

She was lost for words.

With the closeness of his body to hers, Chesca felt as though the only two people in the room were her and Will, wrapped up in a traditional dance that he knew surprisingly well. He was smooth with his feet and kept the rhythm in time with the music.

Rather than retorting with some quick-witted reply, she simply offered a smile and a knowing nod to her partner, and let herself do as he suggested. Enjoy the dance.

After two back-to-back songs, Will offered to find them something to drink, but Chesca wanted to show him the well-dressed coffee bar Abigail had laid out. Besides, she wasn't into consuming alcoholic beverages with so much work ahead of them the next morning.

With the chill of the spring evening, she had a sudden craving for the one thing she really enjoyed about her mother's events. Coffee.

Abigail Thorne made a point to order in specialty coffees from around the country, and a few from around the world. It was interesting to try variations on an old favorite, and since she knew Will enjoyed a cup of java from time to time, she hoped he too would appreciate the variety available to them and try something new.

At the coffee station, they sniffed beans from all the flavors available, and checked out the little write-ups attached to each brew. It was a nice touch to be able to read something about what they were enjoying, and added to the adventure of trying something off the beaten path.

As they sniffed the strong aromas of Kona, Italian and Indian imports and more, Chesca stopped the coffee tour when she spotted a decanter of chicory coffee.

She thought for a moment and Will picked up on her working attitude. "You can't stop working for long, can you?" he joked. "What now? You think of something related to the Cavanaugh family?"

"No," Chesca said, not believing she hadn't thought of it before. "We have to go. I need to call the office in Baton Rouge. I think I just sniffed out a clue as to what our killer there may do for a day job."

Chapter 15

The rental car had been returned and the management had understandably been very pleased to see Chesca this time, as the second car had survived her journey and had been turned in looking much better than the first. She had again apologized for the vandalism, but she also knew her insurance covered any repairs, so she wasn't left with a hefty bill to pay.

Thankfully Will and Chesca were able to find an airline servicing their needs with some open seats, so they didn't have to wait long before making their departure from Boston on the way to see Eric Pace.

While en route, Chesca did some follow-up work with the Baton Rouge team, to see how her theory had panned out.

All it took was a sniff of that chicory coffee from the spring fling coffee bar. It didn't take much for her senses to register the familiarity of it, and within seconds Chesca's mind flashed back to her assault by the killer.

She recalled how he had wrapped his arm around her throat, choking her. And while she picked up pieces of his identity such as her estimations of his height, weight and body shape, she was able to assemble further information.

With his arm wrapped around her neck, she was able to pick up a few scents that at the time didn't mean much.

But now she knew what the combination may have implied and she had called the team leader immediately so they could check out her ideas.

On the suspect's sleeve, Chesca had detected oil, that at the time she supposed was the kind of oil one would find at a mechanic's shop or some other industrial plant.

She also detected the scent of chicory.

And after smelling that coffee, she wondered.

"Is there a chicory coffee factory nearby?" she asked Agent Sharland over the airplane telephone.

"There is," he said, giving Chesca an immediate sense of relief in hearing those words. "And we did what you suggested. Forensics is having a look at the evidence on the victims to see if there is trace of residue that resembles what you described. We know that there was brush-off from when our guy had you by the neck."

"And if the trace evidence is consistent," Chesca said, as Will sat beside her, eager to hear how things were panning out on her open case, "that may be enough to have merit with a judge and provide further proof he's the guy."

If each of the victims had evidence of oil or chicory attached to any of their personal articles, the team would be able to formulate an argument that tied each of those bodies together, lining up the series of crimes and throwing a charge against their guy.

Chesca wanted to know one thing for certain. "You've verified that's where the suspect works?"

It wouldn't be enough to tie the murders to the chicory coffee plant. That would be circumstantial. But, if the suspect was an employee there, it would be a great addition to the already increasing evidence they had against him, and might be the fine line they needed to seal the deal with making a conviction stick.

"He does," Sharland said, "and I've got a car out there now bringing in his personnel files. We'll look at his work schedule, outside calls, materials used by him in his trade. And little by little, we'll be sure to convince a judge that our suspect is indeed responsible for those crimes."

He may have been able to outsmart them with leaving little evidence as to his identity, and though he didn't show up in any fingerprint database, they wouldn't need it. So what if he had never been arrested for any crimes before? That didn't make him immune to being charged with anything he was now guilty of, and it was high time his actions caught up with him.

"I'm glad to hear it," Chesca said, and she meant it.

She'd been frustrated since she'd heard there was a lack of evidence in nabbing her guy.

After she had spent such time profiling his actions, and then risking her life while on the physical hunt for him, she didn't want to let this one slide. She had a solid score keeping tally of successfully closed cases, and she refused to let a little lack of evidence stop her from keeping up her reputation, and putting this man away.

Agent Sharland described what his team was doing and when Chesca should expect to hear some news. "And in case I didn't mention it before, thank you. It was a pleasure to meet and work with you, and now it looks like we're going to have something stronger to work with."

She accepted the compliment and thanks and made sure Sharland would keep her up to speed with any new findings. As she said her goodbyes and hung up, relief filtered through her that at least one thing on her to-do list was getting that much closer to being scratched off for good.

Will elbowed Chesca and smiled. "Hey, good thing we went to your mother's party. See, had we not gone and had a good time, you wouldn't have shown me that cool coffee setup and who knows when or how you would have made that connection."

"I'm just glad it's wrapping up. It was like a bad rash scratching at me."

Will laughed. "Yes, you workaholic. I could tell. But, from what I could tell, that was a successful phone call."

She shared with Will the smaller details of how

Sharland was working the final leg of the case while she was at a distance. Then she took a moment to look at her partner.

"You know, I have to tell you something," she said, wondering if her confession would amuse him or give him cause for worry. "I didn't initially want to have anyone tag along with me."

"Wow, I feel so welcome," Will joked.

"But I'm glad you're here. The company has been nice, and it's nice to know you've got my back," Chesca said, giving her earnest thanks for his accompaniment. "Plus, you're an all-round good guy, Will Evans."

"Aw shucks, you're making me feel all warm and fuzzy inside."

She jabbed his side, laughing at how he was mocking her. "I'm serious. It's been really nice to have the moral and professional support. I suppose I get so used to going it alone out there, I get accustomed to being in a somewhat thankless profession, and it's nice to have someone on your side, rooting for you along the way."

As she said this, Will nodded along, his good old boy, down-South good looks catching a streak of sunshine coming in from the window seat.

Chesca again noted how handsome he was, but more so she was pleased and honored to have developed a good working relationship with Christine's great-nephew. And she hoped she was making a friend she would want to keep in contact with.

Though she didn't know that she would ever have the

opportunity to spend time with Will once this assignment was wrapped up, she knew for a fact she liked his disposition, his friendliness and his views on life.

It was refreshing for her to meet someone and take to them so quickly. From the moment she met him, she could sense Will was an upstanding guy who wouldn't get in her way. And the more she got to know him, the more she liked who he was as a person and what he stood for.

Plus, despite their working relationship, it was nice to enjoy the brief moments of socializing, over meals and dancing at the Thorne Foundation spring gala. With so much of her time focused on work, it was rare Chesca made new friends outside of the job, and those she met on cases were often in and out of her life faster than it took the case to be solved.

Though she didn't know how it would work out, she wanted to make a point to keep in touch with Will. The past few days with him had been relaxed, in spite of being on the hunt for dangerous prey. She was having a good time sharing his company and wanted to have the opportunity to do so again.

"When do you head back out?" Chesca asked, wondering what Will's plans were for returning to his position.

"In time," he said, accepting the water from the beverage cart passing them by. They would also be eating a small meal on board, having caught a flight that would be serving lunch, saving them time from grabbing something on the way to meet Pace. "But for now I plan on relaxing."

"You don't appear to be a guy who gets stressed out over much, how much more relaxed can you get?" Chesca joked.

"I've been at the same thing for years," he explained. "Which I love by the way, don't get me wrong. But it's also been quite some time since I've just kicked back, enjoyed some time off, and now I've got that chance."

Though Will had been on the wounded list for taking a bullet in Iraq for a visiting general, it didn't slow his efforts. A little rest and relaxation was likely all he needed to get pumped back up about going back to work.

Chesca recognized that whatever assignment Will was working on in Iraq or anywhere else, his work was anything but light and effortless. Chesca realized the benefits of knowing when to take a break and using that time to recoup personal and physical strength.

Though she wished she listened to her own reasoning more often.

"So your big plans are?" she asked, wondering how Will would spend his days.

"Back South, spend some time with family. And you can guess I'm going to spending some quality time outdoors. You should try it. Actually, you should come by for a visit sometime."

Chesca felt a rush of awkwardness. She was caught off guard by the suggestion, though she wondered what it would be like to spend time with Will in a nonprofessional capacity. "Me? I've never gone fishing. Or hunting. Except after people of course," she joked nervously.

He gave a hearty laugh. "Oh, you'd love it. There's nothing like the chill of a morning dew to get your blood flowing. The fresh air, getting outside to let the warm morning sun melt your insides and bring you back to nature. It's a trip."

"I can tell you love it."

"I do, and I bet you would too," Will said, and Chesca believed him. The way he described his natural playground was enough for her to want to try it sometime and see if she did in fact enjoy it as much as he suspected she would. "I'm serious, Chesca. When this thing wraps up and you get back to your routine, make a point of asking for some vacation time. You should come out for a week, spend some time out on the water. Hang out with Christine and meet my family. It'd be a great way for you to unload some stress and take a well-deserved break. Promise me."

The request jarred her. Had Will given Chesca an honest invitation? She was flattered, but wasn't sure when or how it would be possible. She knew her workload was ever increasing at the Bureau, and taking time away to work on the Oracle assignment had been one thing. But a vacation?

"I'll try my best," she said, not wanting to promise anything one way or the other. Plus, she wanted to leave room for Will to change his mind, if he was just being polite and making conversation.

But the idea of spending relaxed time with Will and his family made her wonder how well she would mesh with them, and if it would indeed be a vacation or if she would be so intent on being on her best behavior it would seem more like work than play.

She admired Christine Evans and had an incredible respect for her. She had been able to have pleasant and friendly conversations with her this past week, over the phone, but she didn't know if that was a relationship she could see carrying over into a more social arena. This was an assignment dear to Athena Academy, after all, and working circumstances were not always indicative of how social interactions would be. Chesca knew that from once dating a coworker.

But she didn't want to put too much thought into it. The one thing she knew was that Will was a great person to be around, and if she did happen to be in his neighborhood someday, she could see herself looking him up. She just didn't suspect she would go out of her way to make it happen, by taking a vacation with the intentions of spending quality relaxed time with him in his Southern backyard.

"You know what you said before?" Will asked, twisting in his seat to face her more directly. "About being uncertain about working with me, before I arrived?"

"Yes," Chesca said, wondering if she had offended him.

"I'm glad you told me that. I know you get used to doing things your own way when you're out on the job. Same goes for me. And, if you really want to know," he said with a boyish look in his eyes, "I felt the same way."

"What do you mean?"

The warm smile on his face widened and Chesca saw his perfect white teeth. She also took notice for the first time how nice Will's lips were when he smiled. They were full, friendly and curled mischievously into a grin that said he had southern charm running through and through.

"When my great-aunt called me up and asked me to come out to Boston to keep a federal agent safe," he explained. "And she said you were a forensic psychologist?"

"Yeah, what?" Chesca asked, wondering what Will had thought of her in advance.

"I thought, oh shit. I'm going to be spending time with a profiling shrink who wants to interpret my every move, my every word, and I was nervous you'd be a drag, I can tell you that much."

"Geez. Thanks for the honesty," Chesca said, rolling her eyes at the stereotypes.

"Nah, wait, hear me out," Will said, and Chesca gave him the opportunity to continue. "I didn't know what to expect. I had all kinds of crazy ideas rolling through my brain, but I got to tell you…"

"Do I really want to know?" Chesca laughed.

"I have to say, I'm glad to have met you. You're not at all what I was expecting, and I don't think it would have been possible to even think of meeting someone like you. But I did, and here you are, a decent, hardworking, opinionated yet open-minded kind of person and I'm not ashamed to say it would have been a crime not to have met you."

While she agreed that meeting Will was a nice addition to the investigation, Chesca was uncertain how to react to such sentiments.

She had only just met Will a few days earlier, and yet she felt so comfortable with him, so at ease in his presence, that it made her feel sad. Sad, that she wouldn't see him on a regular basis after the case was closed. She, too, agreed that not meeting Will would have been unfortunate, but with their homes being so far apart, and each of them regularly traveling for the purpose of work, she knew keeping up a friendship with him would be a struggle, and she didn't want to get too disappointed by becoming attached to someone she didn't know for a fact that she would see again.

"Thanks, Will," she said, hardening her tone to focus on work and move her thoughts away from how fond she was becoming of her partner. "You've been a great help on this assignment. I appreciate you being here," was all she was able to say.

But Will didn't miss the redirection in her voice. While she had been polite and complimented him as well, it was clear Chesca was doing her best to keep personal matters out of the job and focus instead on their professional relationship.

Chapter 16

While the rest of their flight had been quiet, with Chesca focusing on reviewing her files and Will taking a nap against the support of the window, they again found friendlier ground upon their arrival.

Chesca felt a little awkward for shutting down Will's compliments, but it was in their best interest if they each just focused on the task at hand and kept things nice. Hoping to make a lasting friendship for two people who lived so far apart and worked nonstop was a setup for disappointment. And Chesca didn't like being disappointed, especially when it came to her nonexistent social life.

But as they arrived at the prison grounds to meet with Eric Pace, conversation again picked up in a more congenial manner. The moment had passed, and each of them were eager to make some headway in the case.

Once they'd passed through security, Chesca and Will found themselves awaiting the arrival of Eric Pace.

They had discussed it earlier, and Will agreed to wait in the hall while Chesca handled the one-on-one time with the former Army Chief of Staff.

As she awaited her interviewee, Chesca refreshed her memory of all that Christine had shared with her over the phone. She had said that Pace was manipulative, vindictive and possessed a superiority complex when it came to figuring out what he felt was best for his country. In the ways he handled special operations, Chesca knew he had few loyalties other than to himself and the power trip he developed in his role with the military.

Inside the small cubicle, Chesca took in the stale air and fluorescent lighting, noticing how stiff the room was in its presentation. There was little comfort offered to her, besides the fold-out chair and heavily weighted table between her and Pace.

Not a drop of décor coated this room, but she was familiar with the impersonal vibe in interrogation rooms and knew the sole purpose of such spaces was to get down to business and pose as little distraction to staff and inmates as possible.

If things went her way, she would be in and out of that room in no time, and on her way to track down potential leads in finding Arachne.

After just a few minutes had passed, two guards

found their way into the room, one on either side of the man she presumed was Pace.

He was in his sixties, she guessed, with his gray hair and skin showing minor signs of age. His hair was trimmed short, and he was casually clad in the usual prison garb, making Chesca take note of his true personal appearance, with his wardrobe merely fabric to cover his person.

As he sat down across from her, she noticed the striking blue eyes that were narrow in shape, haunting almost. They were bright but clear, and Chesca felt as though she could see her reflection there.

The two guards took a step back to their post, keeping guard of the room but giving enough privacy for Chesca to conduct her business.

"Pace," Chesca said, keeping her introduction short.

His nod was his reply, and he was clearly showing evidence of being displeased in having to sit through the conversation. He had little choice in the matter, so Chesca got straight to the point.

"You were Marion Gracelyn's CIA handler in Vietnam?" she asked him, though she'd had that information supplied to her earlier by Christine.

"That's right."

Chesca noticed the monotone inflection in his voice, and she suspected he had developed such neutrality over the years of working in special operations. She imagined it was Pace who was often in her seat, interrogating others, and yet the tables were now turned.

"And you were also Jackie Cavanaugh's handler."

Chesca watched as Pace showed little reaction to the last statement, though she could tell the name not only struck a chord with him, but affected him in an unpleasant way. She presumed he held a strong grudge from the past.

"That's right," Pace said, keeping his words to a minimum. He'd no doubt learned it was best to answer with short statements, giving off no more information than that which was requested of him.

But it was a trick Chesca knew well enough on her own. She would use her knowledge to ask the right questions, to lead Pace into giving her what she needed.

"I am aware that you sold out Jackie to Colonel Tom Marker," Chesca said, revealing to him that she knew much of his manipulative history. "Seems you like to make deals, am I right?"

"Depends," Pace said, not shifting in his eye contact with her.

Chesca had files laid out in front of her to use as bait if Pace refused to cooperate. Though she didn't bring in her Oracle information, Chesca made a point to assemble enough documents to make it appear to Pace that she had a stack of info on him that could potentially incriminate him further in other crimes.

It was an old tactic she loved to use.

When face-to-face with a criminal, she made sure to let their imaginations dictate their actions. By using a well-placed piece of evidence—or something that looked like evidence—she knew she could sway the opinion of someone who wanted to claim innocence in a situation.

By having them fear she possessed factual evidence of their crimes, the bad guys were usually that much quicker to make confessions and request deals. It worked for rapists, murderers and other criminals, and Chesca hoped it would work in her conversation with Pace.

If he believed she possessed more background information on him than he would care to share, he might be that much more inclined to share his own viewpoints in defense, thereby giving Chesca information she wanted.

It was worth a shot.

"You know I don't care about your attempts on Monihan," she said, letting him know she had nothing to do with that criminal case. She also wanted to be clear she had no power in lessening any of those charges. Even if she could, she wouldn't agree to make a deal with Pace on his attempt to assassinate the president.

"Then what is it you want?" he asked, heading her off with a direct line of questioning.

"I am looking for someone you are familiar with," Chesca said, meeting Pace's glance with one of determination. "Jackie Cavanaugh was under your command in Vietnam, but I suspect your relationship with her was less than on the up and up."

Again Chesca noticed how Pace was trying to disguise his reaction in hearing Jackie's name.

"What about it?"

She shifted in her uncomfortable chair, and leaned in close to the interview table to make sure Pace understood she held no fear in approaching him, or in discussing topics that clearly made him uncomfortable.

"She was credited with a number of high-profile kills during various missions," Chesca said, setting him up for what she wanted to know. "She was also known to use a signature, is that right?"

"What kind of signature?"

"A calling card. To sign her kills." Chesca stared into Pace's blue eyes to read any dilation in his pupils. "She used a Queen of Hearts playing card, is that correct?"

Though Delphi had shared that information via the couriered CIA files, Chesca wanted confirmation from Pace.

"I suppose she did" was all he said in admission of the fact.

"Good. Now we're getting somewhere." Chesca flipped some pages of her files, and cracked her neck, letting out some tension from the plane ride. What she really wanted was a long soak in the tub to unwind her muscles, but that sort of luxury would have to wait. "I also heard she nearly lost her life, but not in fighting during the war. Care to shed some light on that for me, Pace?"

"I don't see the point of traveling down memory lane with you, Agent," Pace said to Chesca. "After all, there ain't much anyone can do to me now with the time I've been given. What's in it for me?"

Chesca was expecting that. It was a given that Pace

would realize there was little she could do for him, even if she wanted to, and that his exchange of information offered little compensation.

"I understand," she said, "you don't care much for Jackie Cavanaugh. Or, you may also know her by the name Arachne, am I right?"

This time Pace did react, and Chesca was glad to have laid the foundation in getting to the chase. With Pace's disgust in hearing the name Arachne, she hoped it would be enough to fuel his anger and make him share something tangible.

"What's in the past should stay in the past," he said, his voice showing restraint.

"But wouldn't you like to see some justice in the works for Arachne, for the woman who caused you so much trouble overseas?"

Chesca gave Eric Pace a moment to assess his thoughts. She knew he was still holding a grudge against the woman he once worked with, and he was disgruntled that she had managed to get away from him. Chesca could see him consider the topic and weigh his options. He could keep things to himself or hold out hope that someone—if not him personally—could make Arachne pay for her wrongdoings.

They may not have had much in common, but the one similar thread Pace and Chesca shared was their desire to bring Arachne down.

Hopefully, that would be enough of a bond for Pace to trust Chesca's offer.

"She has a long list of enemies," Pace said after taking some time to consider his options. "So you may want to come up with better bargaining tactics."

"Duly noted," Chesca joked back, seeing Pace soften into compliance.

Pace leaned back in his fold-out chair, but his attempts at getting comfortable did not translate into conversation. "Yes, she was nearly killed in Vietnam. Likely more than once, too, since she was known to many, but a friend to few. Can't say she didn't have it coming."

Chesca thought of the information she had gained from the CIA dossier on Jackie Cavanaugh. "You yourself put a hit on her at one time, didn't you?"

Pace nodded his head. "I did. There were so many POWs in Vietnam, trying to get them released was a top priority. We had to do what we could to get our boys out of there."

"So you traded her in?"

"Like a used car," Pace said, letting his distaste for Arachne surface more. "She was a liability. Knew too much, was capable of that much more. She had to go."

"So you exchanged her life for POWs?"

"That was the plan. I tried," Pace said, shaking his head at the failed attempt. "I figured it was a fair trade. She had done her job when we needed her, but then after that she just became a handful. Took on too much power for her own good and was starting to get in the way with some personal agenda of hers."

Through Christine Evans, Chesca had heard how

Eric Pace was a man with a load of political resentment and a streak of dangerous candor. She knew he would do just about anything to have things run as he wanted, and would easily dismiss anyone who got in his way.

"Do you think she was aware of what was going on?"

Chesca knew that if Arachne was aware of the truth behind the attempt on her life, it would have fueled her sociopath mind with thoughts of vengeance and retaliation.

"About the attempted hit? Oh, likely," Pace said, though shrugging his shoulders as if he didn't care about what Arachne knew or didn't know. "She had her ways of finding out information she wanted. And she knew how to make temporary friends, in order to get her own way."

Chesca thought of what she was learning from Pace and added it to her mental store of what she was learning about Arachne's history. Putting together the puzzle pieces of the times and places and the people involved in this tangled web was a headache, with fine details that were not to be overlooked. It could be any little trigger that could lead her to Arachne, and she didn't want to miss a thing.

"How did it go down? The trade-in, I mean," she asked Pace.

"I got in touch with Tom Marker, whom you already mentioned, so you'll know the colonel."

"And what was his role in this?" Chesca asked.

"He was the one who got the trade set up to exchange Arachne's life for two POWs. Shame it didn't work out," Pace said. "I would have liked to have seen her disappear decades ago."

Chesca thought of Pace's bloodlust for Arachne, and despite her disinterest in whatever Pace would have to say about why he attempted to take the life of Gabe Monihan, she was grateful to be able to get additional information from him pertaining to her hunt.

"Do you remember the POWs?" she asked, wondering if perhaps that link would help her in any way.

Pace sat up in his chair, adjusting under the lack of comfort afforded by the stale white-walled room.

"I wouldn't forget such a thing," he said. "Those two guys are stuck in my mind for good."

She got her pen ready to jot down the names, knowing she'd want to do a follow-up to see how their histories intermingled with Arachne's.

Pace took his time in making the statement, but once he did, it was well worth it.

"John Quincy and Cary Banks."

The first name rang a bell with Chesca.

She had heard of John Quincy through the news shared on the Athena Academy Web site, and in conversations with her peers.

Quincy was the man who had made a failed attempt on Athena graduate Josie Lockworth's life.

As Chesca listened to Pace describe his knowledge of Quincy and Banks, she made a note to send information to Delphi to have her connections at Oracle seek out the locations of each of these men.

She knew it would be wise to chat with Quincy to further investigate his connection with Arachne, and she suspected it would be worth her while to locate Banks as well.

Once Chesca felt she'd gotten all she could from Pace, she thanked him for his time. "I do appreciate it, Pace. Like I said, nothing I can do for you in exchange, but hopefully sharing that knowledge did you some good in clearing your mind a bit."

Pace got up from his seat to be accompanied by the guards. "Hey, if you manage to bring down Arachne, that will be payment enough in my books."

"Then it seems we have something in common," Chesca said, as she made her way out to meet up with Will.

Despite having nothing else in common with Pace, it seemed to Chesca that she wasn't the only one who was determined to bring down Arachne, the Queen of Hearts.

Chapter 17

The frequent flyer miles were adding up as Chesca and Will made their second journey of the day. They were tracking down John Quincy.

Pace had revealed his working relationship with Quincy in Vietnam, and Chesca took her time reviewing the findings with Will as their flight touched down in Leavenworth.

"Pace said Quincy was one of the POWs he traded Jackie Cavanaugh in for," she informed him as she assembled her notes and put them in an orderly fashion.

Will led the way to the rental car kiosk in the airport, to pick up the car he had reserved prior to takeoff. "Which means he was a fairly significant accomplice to something, I take it. Or was Pace really that kindhearted?"

Chesca laughed. "Yeah right. More like your first guess," she said, signing her name to the rental agreement and handing over her credit card.

Luckily they had made it on a standby flight and hadn't lost time with their travels. During their flight, while Will handled the car reservations, Chesca was able to send an e-mail to Delphi to let her in on the results of the meeting with Pace. In addition to promising to follow up on any additional information, Delphi made arrangements for Chesca to meet with Quincy at the jail.

During the short drive to the prison grounds, Will took the wheel so Chesca could feed him information from her findings and bring him up to speed.

"Quincy was a U.S. Air Force major general, and that's how he came into contact with Pace," she explained. "He was involved in the Education and Training Command, so you can just imagine his personal capability for getting folks in line for some pretty intense situations."

She knew with Will's military background he was familiar with various posts and assignments, and she didn't need to explain the particulars to him. The army was like a second family to Will Evans, being a career lifer like the rest of his relatives.

"And I suspect he also worked alongside Pace?" Will asked.

Chesca sipped at the lukewarm coffee she had picked up at the airport terminal, and made a mental note to stop for something to eat after their interview with Quincy. It had been hours since they'd snacked on the light lunch provided by their earlier flight out of Boston and the day was fading into early evening. They'd need to refuel to keep up their energy.

"He definitely has something in common with Pace," Chesca said. "He was found guilty of trying to kill the president, like Pace, and he has done some pretty serious sabotage attempts on government equipment."

That was what had happened in his attempts to kill Josie Lockworth, she recalled. Josie's spy plane had been tampered with and it was all credited to John Quincy.

"Since being convicted, he's been serving his sentence, but it won't be over with anytime soon," Chesca said as they found their way past security clearance at the prison yard. "He's got a life sentence in here and with his presidential assassination attempt to his credit, he won't be seeing any time removed for good behavior."

"You want me to come in with you?" Will asked, as the guard led them through a hallway to where Chesca was to meet with Quincy.

"No, it's okay. Wait outside, take a breather, and wish me luck in there."

But Chesca needed more than luck.

John Quincy was not budging. When the guards informed her he was refusing to speak with her, she quickly became anxious that this lead might turn out to be a waste of valuable time.

"You didn't tell him I was a federal agent, did you?"

she asked the guard. She didn't want to make it any more difficult than necessary to weed out information from an inmate who didn't like to follow the law.

"Nope. But he refuses to talk to you, and there's nothing I can do to make him. I'm sorry you've wasted your time."

Chesca refused to be turned away so quickly.

After all, she and Will had just spent a few hours on yet another flight, and there was no way she was going to let this go down as a wild goose chase.

"How about you take me to his cell?" she suggested.

Perhaps if she could get face-to-face with the man, in his comfort zone, she could find a way to get him to open up and converse with her.

"That's not how it works in here. And it's not in your best interest, I'm afraid." The guard crossed his arms in front of his chest, but he spoke to Chesca with an open tone. She could tell he was just doing his job, but she hated that he had to follow the rules. "They'd eat you alive in there."

She knew it was out of the ordinary for this prison. Inside these walls were some seriously gruesome murderers, rapists, thieves, counterfeit scam artists, drug lords and more. But she also knew she was accustomed to working alongside this demographic.

It was nothing new to her.

As Will overheard part of the conversation, he stood up from his seat in the hallway to join the guard talking to Chesca.

"She knows what she's doing," he said, defending her experience with criminals.

"Who are you?"

"I'm her bodyguard. William Evans, U.S. Army."

Immediately, Chesca was caught by the smile the guard donned for the introduction. "Oh, yeah, what's your post? I got a kid overseas right now."

Chesca couldn't believe it. Despite her ability to work people, all it took for this particular jail guard was the notion that he could, on some level, relate to his son that he hadn't seen in years. She recognized that it was the smallest thing that connected one person to another, and no doubt this guy had missed his kid so much, the simple act of meeting a fellow military man was enough to bond him to Will.

As she stood on the sidelines, listening to the half-hour conversation about wars and the guard bragging about his son's dedication in serving his country, Chesca observed Will's mannerisms as he discussed something close to home.

As he spoke, he did so with pride and dignity, revealing how honored he was to do what he did and serve his country, but never once did he fall into telling clichéd war stories or making himself out to be anything special. But Chesca knew Will was special. He had extraordinary talents and had climbed his way up to the very coveted position of protecting generals and higher-ups. He'd had to pay his dues, and yet he had a modesty in his demeanor that Chesca respected and admired.

While they joked about things they could each relate to, the guard warmed up to Will. This small but evidently meaningful connection was enough to loosen his mentality and he turned to Chesca with a forgiving shrug of the shoulders.

"I guess it wouldn't hurt," he said, rattling his keys. "Come on. I'll take you down there, but only for a few minutes. Any longer than that, we'll cause a commotion and they'll have my head."

"Understood, and thank you," she said as she followed him into the cell block. Then she turned her head toward Will and gave him a quick wink. "Nice job. Thank you."

Will shrugged his shoulders as if the gesture was nothing, but to Chesca it meant the difference between seeing John Quincy in person or walking away empty-handed.

Amidst the usual cell-block activities of solitaire card games being played and letters being written, Chesca heard the sounds of conversations being shared between bars and one inmate's dreams being shared with another.

Each of the convicted had their own story to tell, their own life on the inside, and memories of a life on the outside. One such story was being told through an a capella song, an inmate quietly sharing his sorrows in a melodic tune.

The prison was its own city, with a demographic of its own reflective of the lives led here and of those that ended here. Chesca wondered how many of them in the

Leavenworth facilities had family or friends visit, or if they even had rights to such social time.

She knew it varied depending on the crimes committed and the extent of their stay, but she also recognized it would be a long and lonely time to be locked up in here with not even Saturday visitations to look forward to.

When the guard leading their path slowed in front of a cell near the end of the second floor, Chesca braced herself and thought quickly of what she needed to know from John Quincy. If they only had a few minutes to stay in the cell block, she'd want to make the best of the gift she'd been given.

"Quincy," the guard said, rattling the bars across the cell. "You've got company."

Chesca heard a hollow voice from within the concrete block, and when she stepped in front of it to see the man she came to see, he again said, "I don't want company. I already made that clear."

"If you'd just give me a moment of your time," Chesca began, hoping her directness would show him she wasn't here for a lengthy inquisition.

"I ain't talking to you," he said, then he leaned back in his cot to give his back to them and let them know as far as he was concerned the conversation was over.

It wasn't enough to stop Chesca's attempts.

She noticed how fit John Quincy was, and credited that to his role in the army. He would have been constantly involved in physical training, keeping his own body in shape while molding others and preparing them for their new life.

Chesca guessed he was in his sixties at least, likely around the same age as Pace, but his gray hair did little to age his body. He was in good shape, even on the inside of this concrete playground.

"What do you know about Arachne?" Chesca tried, in an attempt to trigger some conversation. "Your life was spared in exchange for hers. Have you got anything to say about that, Mister Quincy?"

There was silence in his cell, except for the slight murmur of a hum. Whether Quincy was talking to himself or carrying on a quiet tune for his own pleasure and distraction, Chesca couldn't tell.

But she did notice his collection of personal belongings taped to the walls.

As he was formerly a highly decorated officer of the army, he had candid snapshots taped up along the wall, accompanied by some awards that must have been given to him when he was respectable and in his prime.

Chesca also noticed envelopes and letters recklessly taped up, indicating that despite his shortness with her, Quincy did have contact with someone on the outside. And it would have meant something to him. Or he wouldn't be keeping the letters as souvenirs.

"Perhaps you can tell me a bit about Tom Marker?" Chesca tried again. "Or Eric Pace. What about Cary Banks?"

She gave a moment's breath in between asking after

each of those names, yet Quincy wasn't budging. He simply laid out in his cot, staring at the ceiling and ignoring the fact that he had company.

After some time had passed, the guard cleared his throat and suggested they call it quits. "I'm sorry, but I don't think you're going to get very far with him today." With a nudge to the air, pointing in the direction of the cell walls hosting all of Quincy's personal belongings, the guard filled Chesca in on some additional information. "In case you weren't aware, this guy has been in and out of psych treatment since the day he got here. He's pretty messed up, you could say, and I don't see him getting better any time soon."

Chesca had wondered about that.

In addition to his obviously personal memorabilia, Quincy had pasted random images cut out from magazines and there were enough newspaper clippings to fill a fireplace. She hadn't been certain whether they were important documents, but now she was getting the idea that he had lost a bit of his sense and was just hanging on to everything and anything that struck his fancy.

She hated failing in this chase. She knew, of course, they still had Cary Banks to speak to and she hoped that would pan out better than their time with Quincy. But she hated to leave a potential informant with no new information.

"What can you tell me about the Athena Academy?" she asked, hoping her one last shot would elicit a response.

And it did.

While she couldn't make out whatever it was Quincy had to say, mention of the Academy had clearly hit a nerve.

His words became louder, though not clear enough for her to decipher their meaning. In fact, to Chesca, it sounded as though Quincy was speaking gibberish, and she found it disturbing that whatever he was expressing was clearly of an evil nature.

The grudge he held against Arachne, and his views on the Athena Academy, were clear. He was not going to open up to her or share a darn thing.

"Okay, time's up," the guard said, steering Will and Chesca away from the cell. "Like I said, this guy is messed up pretty bad. If we don't get out of here now he'll lose it and then the trickle effect will kick in, and next thing you know we'll have a full-out freak show in here."

Though she was disappointed they had come all that way for nothing, Chesca knew when to give in and draw the line. She respected the guard's decision and knew it was in everyone's best interest if she did exactly as he asked, and left before too much of a scene erupted in the cell block.

She had seen these things happen before and the last thing she wanted was to be the catalyst for a big brawl or a long night of watch for the guards.

"I'm sorry there's nothing more I can do for you folks," the guard said. "But it was a pleasure to meet you, and Will, I wish you the best for your next trip. Keep yourself safe."

"I will," he said in reply. "And I wish the same for your son."

Chesca and Will thanked the man and collected their personal handguns from the front security desk as they made their exit from the prison.

"Shit," Chesca said, venting her frustration.

"Hey, you can't win them all," Will said, jabbing her shoulder playfully, then smoothing it down to comfort her disappointment. "You did your best in there and that's all you can do. We'll make better progress with Banks."

"I certainly hope so," Chesca said, though inside she was beginning to wonder if she was ever going to find a solid lead on the elusive Arachne.

The information she had gathered thus far would no doubt be of assistance to Delphi in her mission to put an end to Arachne's web of deception. But to Chesca, her own personal victory wouldn't be had until she herself felt that she had gathered everything she could, and she just wasn't feeling that yet.

They took a moment to group their thoughts, sitting in the parked car outside the prison. The day was coming to a close with the sun beginning to fade against the landscape, and Chesca reminded herself that they needed something to eat.

They had another task ahead of them in meeting with Banks, and it was important they find something to nourish their bodies to keep up their stamina.

"What's the plan?" Will asked, having picked up on Chesca's evidence of thinking on the job again.

"Food. Definitely food. Preferably something with a lot of protein. How do you feel about steak?"

Will laughed as he turned the car back out onto the main road. “You do realize you’re talking to a man who likes to hunt, right? I love any kind of meat and steak sounds great. Any place in particular?”

As they connected to the expressway that led back into the city, Chesca received a text message from Delphi, confirming an appointment had been set up with Cary Banks for the next morning. Only problem was, it meant another long journey.

“Whatever’s on the way to the airport,” Chesca said. “We’ve got reservations for a late-night flight to Scottsdale.”

Chapter 18

They arrived in Scottsdale at three in the morning and had found a hotel close to the airport to settle in for a few hours' sleep so that they would be refreshed for their morning appointment with Cary Banks.

Though the flight wasn't long in duration, it felt like it took forever for them to get to their destination, as three flights in one day was enough to wear on Chesca's body.

Then again, she thought, she *had* been on the road for days. With the back-to-back assignments of her case in Baton Rouge and this one in Boston, she'd been going nonstop and her body was feeling the need to rest.

She knew she could take an extra day or two upon returning home to Richmond, prior to heading back to work. But that would be then, and she wasn't sure how worn out she'd be by that point.

Though the hour was late and she needed sleep, Chesca opted to enjoy a soak in the tub before falling into bed. Her muscles were calling for attention and the hot water would serve her well.

As she lay in the bathtub, letting the heat melt into her skin, she thought of what a run of days it had been for her. In a short amount of time she had managed to get one obligatory family visit off her checklist for the year and had also managed to develop the seeds of a friendship with Will Evans.

Though she was accustomed to interacting with several people during the course of a regular workday, this had been the most socializing she had done in some time. She laughed to herself thinking, it was all a side effect of the assignment she was working on.

"Two birds, one stone," she mused to herself as she slid deeper into the tub.

Despite her disappointment with the nonexistent conversation with Quincy, Chesca was again finding herself in good spirits. Sure, they still had work to do, but she had learned long ago on the job that wishing doesn't make a case go faster. And getting herself worked up over things she couldn't control would only frustrate her, and potentially slow things down.

She knew she would complete her task in time. All she needed to do was be a bit more patient, trust her gut and follow the tangible leads she did have.

Thankfully, Delphi was able to arrange for the quick flight, and set up an appointment with Cary Banks early in the morning. After a decent night's sleep, she and Will would be on their way and start the day off right.

When she drained the water from the tub and finished moisturizing her body, Chesca dressed herself in a T-shirt and boxers and entered the main space. They had decided on sharing one room, with two beds, knowing there wasn't much time to require personal space. And besides, Chesca had reasoned to Will, they were a team and there was nothing odd about the two of them sharing the same space.

She tiptoed into the bedroom area, cautious not to disturb Will. Though he had assured her he would wait up for her, he had passed out and was snoring softly in his bed, the blankets wrapped tight around his waist, exposing the upper part of his muscled body.

Though they had been in close proximity the past few days, Chesca got a good look at Will for the first time. She sat across from him, on the edge of her bed, and allowed her eyes to roam his sleeping form.

Just as much as when he was wearing jeans, Chesca could see Will's in-shape physique, but wearing little more than a pair of boxers, she had been given the opportunity to take in more of his fine frame.

Even though he was sleeping and wouldn't know any better, Chesca felt a bit naughty for watching him and taking the time to appreciate the nearly naked man in front of her.

She was through with denying to herself that she had an attraction to him, and the opportunity to fuel her mind for sweeter dreams was too much of a temptation to resist.

As she lay back into bed, shutting off the sole light beside the bedside table, Chesca let herself drift into sleep, thinking of how well she would like to get to know Will, if the circumstances were different, and they didn't live so far away from one another.

In the morning, Will and Chesca wasted little time getting out of the hotel room and onto the road. Between Will's five-minute shower and Chesca's ability to be speedy with her morning routine, it took them less than thirty minutes to check out of the hotel and pick up some coffee on the way to meet Banks.

After Eric Pace had given a heads-up to the former POW, Chesca found introductory information on her latest find, though she hoped she would have better luck with him than what she had encountered with Quincy.

Cary Banks used to be a flier and an officer in the navy, and she knew he was shot down while in Vietnam. He was one of the POWs brought back by Colonel Tom Marker, and since leaving the navy he'd made a home for himself working as a private investigator. Why he didn't return to his hometown of Phoenix, Chesca wasn't sure, but he had been in Scottsdale for some time now. Chesca and Will were eager to meet with him at a diner across the street from his office.

Pace had shared information with Chesca about his trade-off of POWs; who knows what Banks would be able to share with her. Perhaps he, too, had a secret to confess. Pace said he had spilled information to Tom Marker over a night of heavy drinking, and that's what got him in such a bind with Arachne. With secrets like that, Chesca wondered what she would be able to get from Banks and if he had something equally juicy to share.

"I just want to be sure," Banks said, as they got into conversation at the diner. "I wouldn't be talking to you had it not been for the arrangement I agreed to. So count yourself lucky."

Chesca didn't have a clue what Banks was referring to, but clearly Delphi must have used some negotiation tactics to ensure he would talk.

"I appreciate your time, and your candor," she said, observing his mannerisms and taking in his personality. "I like it when people are direct with me."

She looked hard at Cary Banks, and determined that he was sincere in what he was able to offer, though talking to her wouldn't have been his first choice. Chesca could respect that.

Whatever it was Delphi had set up for him must have been hard to say no to, and thus Chesca had the good fortune of having at least one person available to her to prod for more detailed information.

Banks was a strong man, she could see that in his presence. At nearly six foot, he held a solid posture and didn't slouch in the slightest as he sat across from them at the old school diner where they had ordered their breakfast.

His blond hair was graying, as was his moustache, but his green eyes gave hints of a youthfulness he still possessed and his speech was upbeat and energetic.

At first, Banks gave information to Chesca that she'd already learned through other outlets. He described the conditions he survived in Vietnam, the other POWs he came into contact with, his purpose in being a navy man.

He, too, expressed anger at what had happened, and though Chesca could sense he carried a mild distaste for things he'd been a part of, she also noticed how clearly Banks was trying to start a new life for himself.

"But something just never sat right with me," he said, using his fork to cut through his fried eggs. He had ordered the same as the rest of them, the "sunshine special" which had a hearty helping of eggs, bacon, home fries, toast and a side dish of fruit. It was less healthy than Chesca generally cared to eat, but it certainly felt good going down.

"And what was that?" she asked, slathering her toast with orange marmalade.

"In that whole setup between Tom Marker and Eric Pace, I swear there was more to it than that." Chesca watched as Banks recalled memories and nodded his head as though he was still trying to piece the history together.

"What about it?"

"I swear there was another POW involved, someone who ended up killed."

Pace had left this part out, if Banks was telling the truth, and at this point in time, Chesca had no reason to doubt him.

"Tell me what you know," she requested, eager to gather new information that could lead them in a more solid direction. "Whatever you know can seriously help me out."

"When Quincy, that nut, and I were being set free," Banks recalled, "I'm pretty sure there was a third who got caught up in the mix. I know I had met him prior to that, but my memory is a bit fuzzy as to how it all happened."

Chesca listened carefully, wondering how the third person fit into place. "Do your best."

"In all the commotion," Banks said, "I can't be sure. But someone else got in the mix of things and ended up dead."

"You remember a name by any chance?" Will asked, and Chesca nodded at him, not feeling that he was interrupting. She had wanted to know that for herself and was glad to hear Will's interest in the case.

"Somebody by the name of Bryan Ellis."

Chesca watched Banks as he shared that piece of information. She wanted to measure the way he said it, how his facial muscles reacted as he spoke.

Because she didn't believe it.

Bryan Ellis was a very powerful man.

And he was very much alive.

Chesca knew who he was, as did many others.

Ellis was currently the House Representative, and was making a natural progression to becoming future Speaker of the House. There was no way Banks had properly identified Ellis as a fallen POW. Ellis was alive and kicking.

"Are you certain no other names come to mind?" she asked, hoping that with some time and thought, Banks would come up with a more likely candidate.

"Hey, I've had nightmares of that day for far too long," Banks said, making a point. "I know. I can't figure it out myself either. That's why I warned you, my memory is a bit foggy. But any time I put my mind to it, and relive that moment, it's the name Bryan Ellis that keeps on surfacing. I don't know what else to say."

The one thing that rang true with Chesca was the point of Ellis being a POW. In fact, it had been common knowledge during the election that Ellis bragged about his time in the military, using that as a cheap crutch to get votes. He was proud of being a very highly decorated Vietnam POW.

No doubt Ellis would be singing the same song in the upcoming election next year. He had already gained a hefty amount of public attention, and all the news outlets and political analysts were saying Ellis had a good shot at making a bid for presidential candidacy if Gabe Monihan decided not to run again.

"Even I know Ellis," Will said, equally perplexed by the notion. "And I don't follow politics as much as I should. There has to be an explanation for it."

Chesca knew that Ellis had returned to Arizona after the war. Since then, he had shown evidence of successfully building his political career. It just didn't make any sense.

But from all external appearances, and from what her gut was telling her, Chesca had no reason not to believe Banks. He had no reason to lie to her, and with whatever deal Delphi had made with him, he could stand to lose out on his end of the bargain if his information didn't hold up.

In less than two hours, Chesca had drained Banks of every memory he had of being a POW. He gave her everything he had stored in his mind, and after Chesca felt satisfied he couldn't possibly be holding anything else back, they ended their meeting and thanked Banks for his time.

Though it was unimaginable how the pieces would fit together, Chesca knew she would find out more if she shared her findings with the Oracle network.

Once Banks had left them alone, Chesca and Will took over the diner booth and turned it into a makeshift workstation. As Will checked in with his great-aunt Christine to see what she knew of Bryan Ellis and his background in Vietnam, Chesca sent an e-mail to Delphi, outlining her newfound information and requesting assistance in determining what the official records had to say about Ellis.

"Now what?" Will asked, once he had gotten off the phone with his aunt.

"Now we wait. It won't be long until I get some feedback on the situation, and then we can go from there," Chesca said, knowing she never had to wait long to receive information from Delphi. Whoever that code name represented was one incredible mastermind.

It was an object of fascination, as much as one of itching curiosity, not knowing who Delphi was behind the name. As much as Chesca wanted to know who it was, she understood that such a role meant handling extremely sensitive information and a code name was used as a means of security.

Just the same, Chesca favored the idea that Delphi was someone with superior mental skills, incredible computer capabilities, and no doubt a highly trained Athena grad. It felt like an honor to Chesca to have attended the same school as some of the world's most elite minds and be grouped into the same set of determined individuals.

While sipping coffee and reviewing the case file to date, Chesca answered her phone thinking it was too quick for Delphi to be back in touch already.

She was quick, but not that quick.

"Thorne, you're going to love this," Agent Sharland bellowed from the other side of the line.

It was the team leader from the Baton Rouge case, and Chesca was eager to hear the news considering the positive vibe she picked up in Sharland's voice.

"Tell me something I want to hear," she said, which caught the attention of Will as she spoke with a smile.

"We got him. As much as we can, anyways," Sharland said, shedding some good news on a case Chesca wanted desperately to close. "Each and every one of those victims had trace evidence suggesting they had been in contact with chicory. And most had streaks of oil on their person as well."

"So you can go ahead now with making those charges stick," Chesca said, pleased her recollection had served them well. She was overjoyed at the one small piece of evidence that tied them all together, knowing no judge would see that as purely circumstantial.

"You got it. Good work, Thorne," Sharland said before hanging up.

Will nodded his head in recognition of her success. "I take it that was some good news."

"Very good news. The Baton Rouge case is over and done for me. Seems our man did well at hiding his identity in every way except one."

"But that's all you needed," Will said, proud of what Chesca had put together.

"Exactly. All it takes is one thread of evidence to seal the deal."

It was a moment Chesca wanted to relish.

This was why she did what she did. Her expertise in working tough cases at times felt good, but these moments, when she was able to declare her work on a case done and know that she could be responsible for valuable information gathered, were the best on her job.

Not long after Chesca settled her excitement over the one case, she received an e-mail from Delphi.

Thankfully, the diner had a wireless Internet connection and Chesca was able to access her e-mail account without a problem.

As she read through the information Delphi located

for her under rather quick circumstances, she could hardly believe it.

"Get ready for this," she said to Will as she scanned the intelligence.

"I'm all ears. Hit me."

Chesca loved how involved Will was getting. He was not only her best cheerleader, but he genuinely wanted to see this assignment generate some quality information in ending the nightmare Athena Academy had been subjected to over the years. With his close relationship to the principal, his great-aunt Christine, it was understandable. And it was definitely an attractive trait, seeing a man want what's right for his family and for the school Chesca loved so much.

"To all outward appearances, it was Bryan Ellis that died in Vietnam," Chesca informed Will.

"So how does that work? Clearly he's alive."

"Seems like a Catch-22 for Ellis," Chesca explained. "His father was so intent on seeing his son succeed in politics, he didn't want his life to be in jeopardy."

"But his son made it into politics fine, all right."

"He did. But with his father paying a stand-in to take Bryan's place in Vietnam, Ellis had his life free from any chance of getting into harm's way."

"I sense a but," Will said, tying to follow the line of thought.

"No one thought the stand-in for Ellis would get caught up in the commotion and end up dead."

"Now, wait a minute," Will said, putting the pieces

together. "Ellis has been high and mighty all these years about being a POW in Vietnam, yet he wasn't even there in the first place?"

"Exactly. And because he has been so vocal about his role there, he has to keep up that image for the public eye," Chesca said.

Will sat back into his seat, shaking his head. "And with an election year just around the corner…"

"Bryan Ellis can't afford to have anyone find out the truth," Chesca said, having a hard time understanding the trouble someone would go to in having such a fake life. Both Bryan Ellis and his father were guilty of it, but it was Bryan that had the most to lose.

"So, let me get this right. Ellis wasn't in the war. His father paid off a stand-in who accidentally got killed. Yet Ellis has been shooting off at the mouth about how he survived being a POW and how much pride he has in serving his country, am I following you here?"

Chesca closed her case notes and nodded at Will.

"That's it exactly. And with the campaigns about to begin, Ellis has to know that if his secret got out, he would be a public mockery, and his career would be over."

"Then I guess we better help him make his confession," Will said, angered at the notion that someone would make such a mockery of something he felt so strongly about.

And Chesca agreed.

"Let's go get Ellis."

Chapter 19

Will and Chesca arrived safe and sound in Phoenix. She didn't want to lose any time in finding out the truth behind Bryan Ellis's scam and thus they had driven a rental car straight from their meeting with Cary Banks.

Will sped along in the direction Chesca had given him, as they were on their way to meet with Kayla Ryan.

Kayla was a fellow Athena Academy graduate who Chesca had come to know over the years on account of her great personality and continued involvement in law enforcement. She was destined to make a lieutenant promotion soon, with her stellar reputation at the Youngstown Police Department where she worked within a satellite office in her hometown base of Athens.

An Arizona native, Kayla had a fantastic and

charming daughter named Jazz, who was the result of a teenage affair with an Air Force cadet. They had met in Kayla's senior year, and not long after she became pregnant her lover abandoned her and the child, taking a transfer that sent him out of town. But Kayla had no problem raising her daughter on her own, especially since so many Athenians were happy to see her succeed at such a joyful time in her life.

She had become close with Rainy Miller, who took to Jazz right away and was like an aunt to her. Kayla had also had the help of her parents and siblings, especially when she went off to college to train for her role as a police officer. Between her Navajo background and her commitment to traditions, Kayla had been a great mother to Jazz and had made a great home for them in Athens. And it was Jazz's eyewitness account of the kidnapping that had begun the search for Arachne.

It was Kayla's analytical skills and ability to work swiftly that propelled Chesca to contact her as soon as they knew where they were headed. Kayla agreed to meet with them and join in the hunt for Ellis.

"You don't need to convince me," Kayla had said over the phone, eager to be of assistance. "You know how much I want to see justice for the Academy, and I'd be glad to be a part of seeing it happen."

Ever since the death of her dear friend Rainy Miller, Kayla had been eager to see Athena Academy get past the attacks and ongoing troubles. Having lost her one friend and fellow graduate, she refused to see any more of her classmates subjected to hardship. She'd almost lost her daughter to Arachne as well, so Kayla was eager to join the hunt.

When they reached their destination and were joined by Kayla, Chesca gave a brief rundown of their purpose. Though she couldn't share all the details due to the length of the investigation, she knew giving Kayla a heads-up on Bryan Ellis would help.

"That's pretty big news for politics," Kayla commented, picking up on the severity of the issue.

"And it also sets Ellis up for some huge public disgrace," Chesca added. "Thus, he'd need a pretty big cover-up to keep the media and public in the dark. If his fake-out ever became common knowledge..."

"He'd be crucified by a military court," Will said, agreeing with their plans to take down Ellis and hopefully put an end to the Arachne chase. "He would see the end of his life in politics."

"He's in the city now," Chesca said, as they made their way to the address Delphi suggested they check out. With Ellis on the political handshaking tour, he could have been anywhere, but Delphi suspected he might be found at a hotel that had been charged to his credit card the day before.

Now that she understood the enormity of what Ellis was hiding, everything was starting to make sense. Sharing her suppositions with Kayla and Will, Chesca was in awe at the connection between these political revelations and her assignment to profile Arachne.

It seemed with each turn, this case became bigger and bigger in significance, and it wasn't only about protecting Athena Academy anymore. It was also integral to finding justice for the people of America.

"The thing about Ellis keeping his little secret," Chesca said, "is that he would have gone to any length to keep it hidden. And if my gut is right in this, something tells me he is either working with Arachne, or doing his best to stay clear of her, because if she had any knowledge of such activities..."

"He'd be doomed," Kayla said, and they all agreed.

The three of them traveled together in an oversized Jeep Cherokee Kayla used at the police station. Accompanying them along the road was a convoy of unmarked cars, ready to act as backup if the occasion called for it.

They wanted to make a subtle entrance into the hotel parking lot, and space out the cars so as not to raise much suspicion of their presence. If Ellis tried to flee the grounds, however, he would be surrounded in no time.

Backed by a small army of officers filtering into the lobby, awaiting the command from Kayla, Chesca led the way as the three of them took the elevator to the mezzanine level where a conference was wrapping up session.

With his public profile splattered across the news on a regular basis, Chesca and Kayla immediately recognized their prey when the six-foot man with graying hair and penetrating gray eyes was spotted exiting the room. Kayla informed her officers of Ellis's location and kept them abreast of the direction in which he was headed.

In turn, the trio picked up speed. When the room began to filter out and make a clearance for them, Kayla struck a pose to make their presence known.

"Mr. Ellis," she said in a clear and determined voice. "We're going to have to ask you to stick around."

Ellis was clearly caught by surprise and he immediately looked around to see what his options were. Realizing he had none, as officers filtered in through each of the entranceways, he surrendered the idea of fleeing and waved his hands in the air.

"Okay, I guess I can take a hint. What can I do for you, officer?"

He tried his best to play politics with them, giving off a wide and insincere smile, but Chesca could see he was obviously disturbed by the invasion and he knew his time was running short.

"Have a seat," Kayla said, pulling out a chair for the House Representative after an officer had patted him down to ensure he wasn't personally carrying any weapons. "We have a few questions you'll want to answer for us."

"And if I choose not to?" he asked, showing the bargaining skills he was proud of as a manipulator.

"We could always talk to the media about your time in Vietnam," Kayla said, which was enough to threaten Ellis into nodding his head with understanding.

"Ask away."

"Apparently, your public image is a bit of a facade," Chesca said, taking her turn at the wheel.

"I'm sorry, we haven't been formerly introduced." Ellis glared hard at Chesca, seeming disappointed in something, but trying his best to keep a poker face.

"Francesca Thorne, FBI. I've been assigned to a case—" she began to explain, but Ellis cut her off.

"You're Thorne?"

"Indeed I am. Does my reputation precede me?"

Ellis laughed heartily, but his amusement was not reciprocated around the table.

"I was just wondering how you enjoyed your time in Boston? Make many new friends?"

Will gave Chesca a look of concern, but Chesca didn't want to back down. Was it possible he had something to do with what had happened to her car and hotel room?

"You had me followed. Why?" she asked, taking the direct approach.

"It was nothing personal, you understand. I was unfortunately informed that someone was checking into my business and I don't take well to that," he said.

"Your business?" Chesca frowned, growing angry as she realized she was staring at the man who tried to make her his puppet and potentially endanger her life. "Then you'll have no problem telling us what your business is, will you, Mr. Ellis?"

The room was wide open, a vast conference centre within the hotel, yet the only people in attendance were the police officers lining the edge of the room, and Chesca, Will, Kayla and Bryan Ellis who were all seated at a round meeting table. Peering at him from across the way, she was able to maintain direct eye contact with him and watch his every move.

"You already know my business. Politics."

"And what does that have to do with me being followed? Do I pose a threat to your political career?"

"You do," he said, focusing his eyes on her and leaning forward in his chair to likely appear more intimidating. "If you were up to what I presume you were up to."

Chesca wasn't falling for his games any longer.

"Listen, Ellis, how about we cut to the chase," she said, her emotions fuelling her more proactive tone. "We know you faked your time in Vietnam and we know your stand-in was killed. There is a lot of paperwork that claims you died as a POW. But seeing as you're sitting across from me right now, we know that's not true."

"It's been a big secret to keep," Ellis said, as though he were proud of having fooled the public.

"And I bet it's been even harder, seeing as you're not the only one who knows the truth of what happened in Vietnam."

"Arachne," Ellis said, realizing he had no more options to fall back on. The truth was out.

"Or as you also know her, Jackie Cavanaugh," Chesca said and Bryan Ellis did not disagree. Now there was confirmation of who Arachne was. It was just a matter of finding out where she was located.

"She is aware of what happened," Ellis said, and it wasn't so much what he said, but the words he used that made Chesca light up inside. He said she "is" aware. Not *was*. Meaning, present tense, which would also indicate that both the CIA files and her brother were incorrect.

Arachne was not dead. She was very much alive.

"So how do you keep her quiet, Ellis, or have you made plans to take her out?"

If Jackie Cavanaugh possessed such information about the truth of Ellis's lies, she would have good reason to use her blackmailing skills, knowing what it was worth to him to keep his career alive. The political player would no doubt succumb to any of her requests, desperate to keep his secret out of the public eye.

"I pay her off," he said, and Chesca made sure to take note of whatever information Ellis could give them. If there were regular payments being made, or interactions conducted between the two of them, they'd be able to set it up so that they trailed Ellis the next time he was to meet Arachne, or at the very least uncover her location through his business with her.

As Ellis described the arrangement he had made with Arachne, Chesca multitasked, thinking how all of her efforts were morphing into something bigger.

Initially, she'd been sent by Delphi to profile Arachne, to determine whether she was one and the same as the Queen of Hearts. Having come to the conclusion that through her signature, the Queen of Hearts playing card, the CIA operative with the code name Weaver—Jackie Cavanaugh—had used that same calling card as Arachne.

In a matter of days, Chesca had uncovered the fact that Jackie Cavanaugh, mob daughter, had several different aliases and that through her various ambitions in bringing down Athena Academy and pursuing her personal agenda, she had managed to gain a great deal of power over some pretty significant public figures and army professionals.

Now, faced with the knowledge that she was blackmailing a potential president elect, Chesca knew that whoever Arachne was at any given moment, she knew how to handle herself and get her way.

In the pursuit of information, Chesca was not only learning the personal makeup of Arachne, as Delphi had requested of her, she was also learning new and key elements in what seemed to be a decades-long conspiracy against Athena Academy. Finally, Chesca was beginning to feel as though her assignment was successful, and she could report back to Delphi with pride.

When Ellis failed to provide the details they desired, however, and skirted the issue with as many generic comments as possible, Chesca dug in with some extra determination. She would not let him get away with politicking her.

"I need details, Ellis," she warned. "We know there's more to it than you're letting on, and if you don't supply a more direct personal connection to Arachne, all it will take is one phone call to the media."

She waved her cell phone as bait, and Ellis gritted his teeth.

"I need some sort of deal," he said, giving up on his perception that he might get out of the conversation untouched. "I'd like to preserve as much of my dignity as possible."

"We'll make deals later," Kayla said.

"I'd rather make one now, if it's all the same to you. I know you know enough to put me away for life, and I know you have enough information in hand to walk out of here and ruin my political career. I need some sort of insurance policy that my entire life won't end today."

"First off," Kayla said, "you're the only one responsible for the demise of your career. You should be ashamed of yourself. You have no one to blame but yourself. But you have my word that we'll arrange for a lesser penalty, if you can give us something to work with, something we don't already know."

Chesca gave Kayla a nod of thanks, and then made eye contact with Will. She was proud to have been in such good company, working alongside some of the best people she'd ever met. And thinking of that reminded her how she had only just met Will a few days ago, and it was only a matter of time before he exited her life and went back to his own once this case was closed.

Though she offered a smile to return his, a pang of hurt filled her. She would miss him, having grown so fond of him in recent days.

"I don't know where you'll find Arachne," Ellis said, and from his tone and facial expression, Chesca was sure he was telling the truth. "I don't have direct contact with her. I make my payments to an account and once the money is deposited, that's the end of it for me, until the next time."

"Then what do you have as a bargaining chip, Mr. Ellis," Kayla said, holding firm that they wanted something more from him.

"I've been employing a computer hacker. Someone I am hoping can do what you aim to do. Find Arachne and put an end to the blackmail, though of course my reasons for doing so are far different than yours."

"How do we get in contact with your employee?" Chesca asked, wanting to get a move on to the next step.

"I make a deal with you," Ellis said, looking at Kayla, "and I'll give you some more information on Diviner."

Chapter 20

Though Ellis provided the name of his computer cracker, Diviner, Chesca suspected he was withholding additional information. More than half of what she learned during an investigation was in what her prey didn't say, as evident with her serial case from Baton Rouge.

Ellis might have tipped them off with a name, but there was more to it than that. And Chesca vowed to find out as much as she could when sealing her assignment shut.

Kayla had agreed to handle the final negotiations with Bryan Ellis so that Chesca and Will could get on the road. They had a few things to check into, and Will wasted no time in hopping into the driver's seat.

"It really irks me," he said, "that Ellis sent someone on your trail to bring you down."

Chesca agreed. Ellis had confessed to aiming to put a halt to her quest to find Jackie Cavanaugh by sending someone to throw her off her course. With that information in her possession, she reminded herself that she'd want to put a call in to Waters to give him a heads-up for his investigation.

Whether or not he'd be able to prove Ellis's involvement would be determined, but if they had any trace on the man who fled the burning car, they could potentially pit him against Ellis in making for a bigger case. One thing was for sure, even with the deal he'd made with Kayla Ryan, Bryan Ellis would be going down.

"I'll send Delphi an e-mail from the plane," Chesca said, as they made their way to the airport. "Once we get to Alexandria, Virginia, we're scheduled to meet Allison at the Oracle office. I know she'll be great at helping out with this next leg of the race."

Chesca had given Allison Gracelyn a quick call to request her assistance. She knew her Athena Academy friend would be able to help in digging up some secretive information over the Internet, and Allison had agreed to make the trip to meet them at the Oracle office.

Though Chesca had spoken with Delphi, she knew not to expect any personal contact with her. Delphi never made a public appearance to secure her anonymity, but Chesca had given her all the information she had to date and would then follow up with whatever she and Allison could uncover.

"I don't like saying it," Will said, keeping his eyes

on the road ahead. "But I kind of feel like I have to just the same."

His tone worried her. "What's that?"

"I don't think you need me anymore. I mean, you've got a profile on Arachne, hands down. And heck, you may even be able to direct your people to where she's hiding out if they can figure out the connection of this Diviner character. So, I'd say, from the looks of it, your job is just about done. Which means, so is mine."

Chesca was silent for a moment as she absorbed what her partner was saying. It was true, she realized, but she hated to admit it to him, and mostly to herself.

She had warmed to Will faster than she'd connected with anyone, and she knew once he'd gone back to his home and she'd gone back to hers, she'd miss having him around and sharing in his company.

"It won't be a problem for you to come to Oracle," she said, trying to convince him he was still welcome.

"That's your job." He briefly glanced at her in the rearview mirror, then returned his vision to the road. "But, how about we compromise?"

"What, you pick up on how to make a deal from Ellis?" she joked, wondering what he had in mind.

"I'll see to it that you make it to Oracle safe and sound, and then I best be on my way. Once you're inside there, I know you're close to being done and I don't want to be a distraction."

"Okay," Chesca said, thankful to have a bit more

time with her newly acquainted friend. "But Will, you haven't been a distraction yet. It's been good to have you around. And I might even go so far as to say—"

"We could be friends?"

"Yeah," she said, happy that he had evidently been thinking the same thing.

For the remainder of the drive to the airport and for the duration of the flight, Chesca and Will had little conversation between them. The silence was comfortable, and it was as though they each wanted to revel in the last few moments they had together by respecting it with quiet comfort.

But as their journey came to a close, with only a few miles between them and the Oracle office, Chesca found herself becoming a bit more chatty.

"So, tell me Will. When is fishing season?"

She had hoped her coy return to the subject he loved so much would be bait for his curiosity, and her bait was met with success.

"Fishing season? Well, there really isn't one."

Immediately, Chesca felt a wave wash over her of disappointment and embarrassment at not having the slightest clue about the sport. "Oh," was all she found herself able to say.

"However," Will said, his voice optimistic and playful, "since everybody back home fishes just about every day of the week, including Sundays, you'd have no problem finding a suitable instructor if you're looking to learn."

She felt her cheeks warm and this time the girlish embarrassment faded quickly with happiness.

"It's possible," she said, though not wanting to make any promises. Between finishing up this assignment and getting back to her regular routine, Chesca didn't know when she would manage a span of vacation time. But she knew for certain she didn't want to leave things at a standstill with someone she had grown quite fond of in such a short amount of time.

She thought carefully as she spoke, wondering if she was being too bold in her intentions. "I don't know when or how I'll manage time away from work again," she said, "but I'd like to think I'll have the opportunity sometime to visit your favorite places, whether fishing or hunting or whatever is in season at the time."

"You hunt?" he said, laughing with that sweet chuckle she had come to enjoy. "Heck, why am I surprised. You hunt every day, it's just for people."

As he parked the car alongside the road where Chesca would soon be making the rest of her journey on her own, Will removed his seat belt and faced her as he shifted in his seat.

"I would enjoy that very much," he said, his voice softer than she was accustomed to. "Francesca Thorne, it has been a pleasure working with you, sharing time with you, and getting to know you. Heck, I even enjoyed that fancy party your mother threw for her fund-raiser."

Chesca laughed thinking how Will had been dragged into the world of the Thorne family. It was enough he unexpectedly got a call from his great-aunt Christine to work as a bodyguard, but Chesca could guess he had little foresight into what the few days would hold, flying from state to state in a pursuit that seemed like it was never going to end.

"You keep dancing like that, and I bet you'd be welcome to attend any social event hosted by my mother. You have some fancy moves, mister," she said, letting her voice flirt with him.

"I sure hope so," he said, adjusting further in his seat, and raising a hand to caress the side of her face.

The contact threw Chesca, but she was not about to argue about whatever Will had up his sleeve. His hands were too warm, his eyes too beautiful and blue, and his words music to her ears.

"Because I can't let you leave me without this," he said, just as he leaned in to give her a very gentle, but very welcome, kiss on the lips.

She felt his warm breath against hers and her heart warmed, too, deafening her with the pulse of its beat. It had been far too long since she had been kissed, and never had she been kissed like this. It was as though his lips were meant to mingle with hers, and for the momentary lapse in time she allowed herself to think of nothing but enjoying his gesture.

When the lights of an oncoming car lit up the interior of their rental, Will pulled away from Chesca in a smooth movement that made him appear as if he were floating away in slow motion.

Chesca said nothing, but let out a slight purr of pleasure.

"That looks like your friend?" he asked, directing her attention to the figure Chesca identified as Allison.

"It is," she said, and despite being happy to see Allison Gracelyn, and eager to get on with their assignment, she knew her time with Will had come to a close.

"Then…"

She nodded her head. "Then it's time for me to go."

Will got out of the car to help Chesca unload her belongings from the back seat and carry them to the edge of the sidewalk. After her work at Oracle was through, she'd be on her way back to Richmond, and she had everything in order for the journey, except the plane ticket she would grab on the way.

"Tell me you'll visit," Will said, wrapping an arm around her waist as they walked across the street.

"I will."

"Tell me it will be soon," he begged playfully, and Chesca smiled up at his six-foot frame.

"As soon as possible," she said. "And in the meantime, you know my number. I hope you put it to use."

Though she didn't want to set herself up for disappointment, Chesca knew there was something brewing between her and Will and she didn't want to let time or distance stop that from happening.

"You know I will," he said. "I can't imagine what my day will be like tomorrow, without you. You're easy to get used to, you know. It just won't be the same without running from airport to airport."

She jabbed him in the side, laughing at his cute jokes. "Good. Then we'll keep in touch."

"I promise you we will," he said, and Chesca believed him.

After one more prolonged embrace, she finally let Will walk away from her and she watched him as he drove off to return the rental car and head back to his outback playground. Had she been told a few days ago that everything in her world would be changed by meeting one person, she wouldn't have believed it. But Chesca knew, without a doubt, that things would be changing. And she knew that was something incredible to look forward to.

As she met Allison at the front of the town-house lawn, she found herself smiling.

"Thanks for coming, Al."

Allison Gracelyn had an impressed look upon her face. "That looked cozy. Care to dish?"

"Maybe later," Chesca said, letting her friend see the joy in her eyes. "But I think we need to get some business taken care of first."

"Ah, you're no fun," Allison joked, and then led Chesca down the pathway to the back door entrance.

There had been only one occasion where Chesca had been at the Oracle office. It was shortly after she had been recruited. It had been a routine visit to get her acquainted with the low-key, but high-security residence.

In the front, Chesca had to pass through a security gate, which she was able to do with ease, knowing the passwords. At the back entrance, both Allison and Chesca were subjected to another screening, with the thumb print and retina scan, making sure they were each privileged with access to the house only Oracle agents had entrance to.

Once inside, they made their way through the homey kitchen, and Chesca dropped her bags there to deal with later. Following Allison's lead, they traveled down the hall to the library, which had computer access for them.

"We've got it set up so we can do some additional searching," Allison said, having made a call to Delphi herself after Chesca had invited her on this last bit of the investigation.

Chesca knew Allison was aware of the Oracle network, and since it stood for so much of what her mother Marion fought for, she knew she could trust her fellow Athenian.

They sat down side by side as Allison began typing code and accessing information Chesca could barely keep up with. She was good with computers, as much as she needed to be, knowing how to use most programs and get around the Internet, but it was Allison who was more skilled in cryptic terminology and Chesca was impressed with her maneuverability skills.

Within moments, Allison had found a way to access the personal computer belonging to Bryan Ellis.

Chesca had shared her concern that he had been hiding more than he was letting on, and they intended to uncover whatever they could through a patch into his personal files.

Though his files were protected with government security, Allison had bypassed that within minutes. Anything he stored in private was made available to them through the software provided by Oracle.

Chesca was truly amazed at what the organization had access to.

Tapping into his files, Chesca suggested they look into his accounting and banking information. "He said he had an employee by the name of Diviner who handled things for him, but I think there's more to it than that."

"There is," Allison said within moments of opening the financial records. "Look at this."

Chesca scanned the information in front of her and could hardly believe it. "He's been making payments into the same Puerto Isla bank that Salvatore Giambi used?"

"And how much do you want to bet that it's the same account number?"

Chesca scoped through her written notes to see what they could match up. For the past forty years, Giambi had been making monthly payments to a Puerto Isla bank account, paying off Arachne. If the account Ellis was using implied the same thing, there was an automatic connection that more was at work here than she'd thought when she was first assigned the case from Delphi.

"The numbers match up," Allison said, showing little sign of being affected by the news. But Chesca knew Allison was all business at this point, using her fingers on the keypad to work as fast as she could to bypass any chance of someone realizing they had tapped into Ellis's computer illegally.

"I have to get this information to Delphi right away," Chesca said, looking on her person for her cell phone, but realizing she'd left it in her handbag on the kitchen counter. "Hey, I'll be right back. Holler if you need me in the meantime."

Allison continued to peruse Ellis's files as Chesca went downstairs and sought out her cell phone. She dialed access to Delphi, wanting to make an immediate call to let her know the connection between Ellis's and Giambi's bank accounts.

"Hi, it's Chesca," she said when Delphi answered. "I've got the latest update."

As she filled in her connection, Chesca couldn't help but wonder who Delphi was behind the disguised voice. Perhaps Allison knew, but it was wrong of her to ask her friend. Even if Allison did know, it was something she'd feel embarrassed about, in trying to find out information that she should only have confirmed by one person.

When she had given the latest to Delphi, she listened to Delphi's instructions on how to get the paper files she had handled back to her. It was policy that Chesca leave every trace of the investigation behind, so as not to create an unnecessary paper trail out in the working world. Oracle handled too much sensitive information to leave things to chance.

After she wrapped up her conversation with Delphi, Chesca made her way back down the hall to the library. When she entered and rejoined Allison, she took her seat and something caught her eye.

Allison's cell phone.

She couldn't recall if it had been laid out on the desk before, or if she was just letting her imagination get the better of her. But, despite her earlier hesitation, Chesca now had the courage to ask.

"I called Delphi," she said, taking her time broaching the subject.

"Good. I've scanned through some more of Ellis's account information, check amounts and dates of deposits. That'll be useful to her."

"To her?" Chesca asked, making direct eye contact with her friend and coworker.

"To Delphi."

Chesca bit her bottom lip, wondering if it was a mistake to ask. But she had to, or she would regret not taking the chance while she had the opportunity. "Allison. I'm sorry to ask you this, but…you're just so good at all this—" she again hesitated for a moment and then got straight to the point. "Are you Delphi?"

Knowing full well how to read expressions, register vocal pitches, and detect fluctuations in either, Chesca had to say Allison gave the most reliable face ever when she shook her head and denied the idea. "Sorry, Chesca, but although I'm thankful for the compliment on my work, you'll have to keep up the guessing game. Besides, you know that for everyone's safety you can't know who Delphi is. And we shouldn't even be discussing it."

"I didn't mean—" Chesca began, eager to apologize for her professional faux pas. She had made an agreement with Delphi, upon signing on as an agent, that she would not seek out the identity of any other agents or of Delphi, and with one question Chesca felt she had damaged part of her oath, but Allison made her feel better within seconds.

"Hey, no worries, people get curious about what they don't know. You know that," she said, dismissing any feelings of unease Chesca had begun to feel. "No way, check this out."

With that part of the conversation clearly over, Chesca settled back into her seat next to Allison and followed her line of sight to see what had come up on the computer screen.

"I didn't realize we'd logged on to Ellis's instant message service in the process of getting into his computer," Chesca said, upon seeing a dialogue box pop up.

"Me neither, but am I ever glad we did," Allison said. "See the sign-on name?"

She did and recognized it, though she wouldn't have one day earlier.

On the instant message sent to Ellis, was a dialogue box with conversation sent by Diviner.

"Do you reply? Ignore it? What are you going to do, Allison?"

Chesca shifted in her seat as her co-conspirator began typing to Diviner asking to meet up ahead of time to make the next transaction. Chesca could see Allison's attempts at posing as Ellis, aiming to entrap Diviner into meeting them at a location they could agree on.

But it wasn't working.

Shortly after hitting send on her instant message, Allison let out a sigh of frustration. "He knows it's not Ellis. He just shut that conversation down. Give me that pen, would ya?"

Chesca did as was requested of her and Allison jotted down the time. 4:30.

As she began typing into the Oracle network, hoping to track down the location of Diviner, aiming to find where the last computer signal ended in his attempts to contact Ellis, Chesca saw something in another open window.

"Allison, you have to see this," she said, angling toward the computer screen.

As they watched from the connection they had to the Puerto Isla banking site, they saw the numbers draining. Someone was clearing the account.

"Could that have been Diviner?" Chesca asked, wondering how it was that Ellis's employee could have made such a move so quickly.

"Perhaps. But not likely. I suspect it was someone Diviner could feed info to rather quickly."

Chesca couldn't believe it. Just like that, the money was gone. "So that's it. Can you trace it?"

Allison shifted her chair away from the computer

station. "Something tells me this is going to take more work. I'll get in contact with Delphi, tell her what happened and when, and she'll get another agent on it. Someone who knows how to dig up the right information."

"I just wish I was able to see the final results," Chesca said, realizing her role in the investigation had come to a close.

"You know just as well as I do, Chesca, that this is far from over," Allison said. "But you should feel good about all that you've been able to accomplish in just a matter of days. You collected some key information and both Oracle and the Athena Academy will be grateful for all you've done. Be proud."

Chesca accepted the thanks for her input into the investigation. She wanted so much to see her findings have an impact on the case.

But she realized she had done her job. She had profiled Arachne, determined her to be the Queen of Hearts, and as an added bonus, she was able to find out damaging information about what Bryan Ellis had been hiding from the public for all these years.

Though it was bittersweet to realize her role was over, she knew her task had been a success. Partly, in thanks to Will for his assistance, and she would be sure to remind him of that when she spoke to him to arrange for some vacation time.

But for now, the rest of the case went back to Oracle, and whoever Delphi chose to follow the Puerto Isla lead would bring them one step closer to bringing down Arachne, and bringing justice for the women of the Athena Academy.

* * * * *

Don't miss the next Athena Force adventure,
BREATHLESS by Sharron McClellan.
Available February 2008.
Turn the page for a sneak preview.

U.S. Marine Corps combatant diver Jessica Whitaker checked her watch. Right on time.

Opening the case attached to the front of her diver propulsion vehicle, she pulled out the explosive device. Flicking on a small, pencil-sized light attached to her helmet, she checked the mine. It wasn't much. A small charge, since this was a training exercise, and they didn't want to actually blow a hole in the ship.

Or a recruit.

She handed the device to Latham. "Tell me what you know."

Flipping on his light, he turned the cylinder over in his hands. "Limpet mine. Magnetic. Capable of a range of charges and producing a range of responses from barely noticeable to *what the hell, there's a hole in my ship.*

She chuckled at his description, but nodded in approval. "Time to get away before it blows?"

Latham examined the timer. "Anywhere from three seconds to three hours, depending on the required settings."

"Give me fifteen minutes," she said, even though the explosion would be little more than the equivalent of a child's cap gun and fifteen seconds was plenty. In a real-life situation they'd need those fifteen minutes, and she preferred to treat this as real as possible even though it was a teaching situation.

Latham set the charge, and in the small line of light from his mask she saw him freeze. "What's wrong?"

He shook his head. "I'm not sure. I entered the correct numbers, I swear, but the countdown is starting at sixty seconds."

"Hand it over."

He handed her the mine, and she punched in an abort code. Nothing happened. *Fifty seconds.*

She punched it in again. Still nothing.

She'd have to speak to someone about this equipment. Whoever was supposed to maintain it was doing a lousy job. Irritated, she took the all-in-one tool kit from her belt and flipped out the Phillips screwdriver.

The screws turned. And turned. But otherwise didn't move outward. They were stripped. She brought the explosive device closer to her mask and noticed scratches around the outside of the case, with the majority being around the screws.

Underneath her tight black wet suit, the hairs on the back of her neck strained to rise as she realized the problem with the timer was not accidental. Quite the opposite.

Sabotage.

Then true horror washed over her. If someone had taken the time to change the timer and strip the screws, then it was a sure bet there was a reason.

Like blowing a huge hole in the ship.

Which meant a larger charge. "Oh, my God," she whispered.

The console blinked the countdown. *Twenty-five seconds.* She dropped the mine, pushing it toward the bottom of the ocean and away from the ship, herself and her trainee. "Latham, get to the DVP and get moving. Now!"

He swam over to the idling machine and set it in motion. The engine sputtered, stopped. He pushed the start button. Still, nothing happened.

Her heartbeat pounding in her ears, Jess pushed him aside and pounded on the console. "Start, you bitch." The machine refused to engage.

Perhaps this was a bad joke, she told herself. Taylor hoping to make her late for the rendezvous so he could win their ongoing bet of who bought the beer.

The bitter taste of fear in her mouth told her differently. "Taylor, you there?"

There was no reply, but neither did she expect one.

Mission protocol, after all. Damn. "If you can hear me, get out of here. We have a problem," she shouted into the microphone.

She prayed Taylor and Eielson were where they were supposed to be. *Sushi* was a big ship. They would be fine unless the charge was so big it disintegrated the entire ship.

However, she and Latham were much too close. "Swim," Jess said to Latham. "Fast."

Latham followed her into the dark water away from the ship, the minuscule beams emanating from their flashlights a thin, bright path in the dark void. "Ma'am, what's wrong?" he asked, his drawl more pronounced than she'd ever heard and his breathing hurried and harsh in her earpiece.

Fifteen seconds. They weren't going to make it. "I'm not sure," she lied. "Just swim."

She pumped her legs, and within seconds was ahead. No one was better in the water. She'd never lost a race in school or since she's joined the marines.

If left to herself, she might even outrace the explosion. Maybe.

But that would mean leaving Latham. A trainee. A young man who trusted her to be a commander and do the right thing.

The right thing did not mean leaving a man behind to die.

She slowed, grabbed his arm and pumped her legs again, pulling him along beside her. He was heavy, slowing her. She refused to let go. He was not going to die. Not here. Not like this.

Neither was she.

"Ma'am, we're not going to make it," Latham said, his voice laced with fear.

"Yes, we are, and Latham, stop ma'am-ing me," Jess snapped.

Behind her, the limpet mine exploded.

Definitely bigger than a cap gun.

Next to her, Latham's eyes widened in fear. Her gaze shifted, adjusted, and she saw her reflection in his mask. Her dark eyes were wide. Panicked. Then the percussion wave rolled over them, tumbling them in its wake. Someone screamed, and for a brief, agonizing second she thought her head would explode. Blackness claimed her, and she sank into the dark.